For Jenny, my love

Acknowledgements

The editor is grateful to the following for permission to use copyright material in this book:

Brian Lumley for *The Viaduct*. Copyright 1976 by Brian Lumley.

R. A. Lafferty and his agent, Virginia Kidd, for *Fog In My Throat*. Copyright 1976 by R. A. Lafferty.

Daphne Castell and her agent, Virginia Kidd, for *Christina*. Copyright 1976 by Daphne Castell.

Joseph F. Pumilia and his agent, Kirby McCauley, for *The Case Of James Elmo Freebish*. Copyright 1976 by Joseph F. Pumilia.

David Drake for *The Hunting Ground*. Copyright 1976 by David Drake.

Manly Wade Wellman and his agent, Kirby McCauley, for *The Petey Car*. Copyright 1976 by Manly Wade Wellman.

Robert Aickman for *Wood*. Copyright 1976 by Robert Aickman.

Ramsey Campbell for *The Pattern*. Copyright 1976 by Ramsey Campbell. Thank you, he said, shaking himself by the hand.

Fritz Leiber for *Dark Wings*. Copyright 1976 by Fritz Leiber.

THE FAR REACHES OF FEAR

edited by
Ramsey Campbell

Star
A STAR BOOK
published by
the Paperback Division of
W. H. ALLEN & Co. Ltd

A Star Book
Published in 1980
by the Paperback Division of
W. H. Allen & Co. Ltd
A Howard and Wyndham Company
44 Hill Street, London W1X 8LB

First published in Great Britain by W. H. Allen

Copyright © Ramsey Campbell 1976

Printed in Great Britain by
Richard Clay (The Chaucer Press) Ltd, Bungay, Suffolk

ISBN 0 352 39513 3

This book is sold subject to the condition that it shall not,
by way of trade or otherwise, be lent, re-sold,
hired out or otherwise circulated without the publisher's
prior consent in any form of binding
or cover other than that in which it is published
and without a similar condition including this condition
being imposed on the subsequent purchaser.

Contents

	page
EDITOR'S INTRODUCTION	9
THE VIADUCT Brian Lumley	11
FOG IN MY THROAT R. A. Lafferty	31
CHRISTINA Daphne Castell	46
THE CASE OF JAMES ELMO FREEBISH Joseph F. Pumilia	66
THE HUNTING GROUND David Drake	75
THE PETEY CAR Manly Wade Wellman	97
WOOD Robert Aickman	112
THE PATTERN Ramsey Campbell	140
DARK WINGS Fritz Leiber	161

Introduction

This is how I edited the book. I asked the contributors, or their agents, to provide the most horrifying or most terrifying story they could. There were to be no taboos, except that the stories must not have been previously published; if they were unpublishable elsewhere, so much the better. I hoped such a book would be powerful; I think it is, not least because the stories trigger the imagination.

Some horror anthologies have contained little more than monotonously gloating descriptions of human maltreatment and sadism. I believe this is pornography without sex – or rather, pornography whose label 'horror fiction' the reader can use to reassure himself he isn't really perverse. The characters are incredible puppets; the writing is immature and unskilled – much as in most pornography. It may be healthier to supply such fiction than to force the readers to seek solace elsewhere. But it is presumptuous to claim that it's horror fiction.

There is none of that sort of thing here. Perhaps that was a taboo. There is gruesomeness, certainly, but not at the expense of the rest of the story: these stories – even given the satirical exaggeration of some – are about human beings. Nor are the characters comfortably distanced by history; nor are the settings. This is not a comfortable book.

What particularly pleases me is the variety of horrors. There's a ghost story poised on the edge of dreadful tragedy. There's a night-mare of vertigo; there's a night-mare of mysterious abductions and their cause in an American suburb. There's a grim fairy tale for adults; its sly terror accumulates on every reading. There is the patch of countryside which may reveal what man means to the universe, and the machine which is unnervingly true to old folk-tales. There's a little comic relief, a parody of the spectral revenges often found in horror comics, which manages to be simultaneously gruesome and funny. There's a terror which may come from deep in the mind, but which is absolutely physical. And there's a tale about nothing less than the single source of all our worst night-mares. I don't intend to say which story is which; it's not my job to spoil your enjoyment.

August Derleth once said he thought anthologies of unpublished fiction were generally inferior to reprint anthologies, because the editor's choice was more limited. But doesn't it depend rather on how stringently one edits? I rejected more than twice as many stories as I bought – and that isn't meant to denigrate some fine tales that simply weren't right for this book. I wanted the book to be all you thought it was promising when you bought it. I hope you aren't disappointed; and I hope to offer you a companion volume soon.

Ramsey Campbell

The Viaduct

by

BRIAN LUMLEY

Brian Lumley (1937–   ) joined the British Army in 1958, and is still in the Army, in Edinburgh. In 1967 he began to write Lovecraftian fiction, encouraged by August Derleth, and is now the most prolific writer still working that vein (in short stories, including a collection The Caller of the Black *; and in several novels, such as* The Burrowers Beneath, Beneath the Moors, *and* The Transition of Titus Crow).

To Lovecraft's ideas Lumley brings a robust enjoyment of storytelling and adventure, and a strongly English style. But his best work doesn't depend on Lovecraft. There is no Lovecraft in this story, but there's a ruthless nightmare, of a kind most of us must admit.

Horror can come in many different shapes, sizes, and colours; often, like death, which is sometimes its companion, unexpectedly. Some years ago horror came to two boys in the coalmining area of England's north-east coast.

Pals since they first started school seven years earlier, their names were John and David. John was a big lad and thought himself very brave; David was six months younger, smaller, and he wished he could be more like John.

It was a Saturday in the late spring, warm but not oppressive, and since there was no school the boys were out adventuring on the beach. They had spent most of the morning playing at being starving castaways, turning over rocks in the life-or-death search for crabs and eels – and jumping back startled, hearts racing, whenever their probing revealed too frantic a wriggling in the swirling water, or perhaps a great crab carefully sidling away, one pincer lifted in silent warning – and now they were heading home again for lunch.

But lunch was still almost two hours away, and it would take them less than an hour to get home. In that simple fact were sown the seeds of horror, in that and in one other fact – that between the beach and their respective homes there stood the viaduct . . .

Almost as a reflex action, when the boys left the beach they headed in the direction of the viaduct. To do this they turned inland, through the trees and bushes of the narrow dene that came right down to the sand, and followed the path of the river. The river was still fairly deep, from the spring thaw and the rains of April, and as they walked, ran, and hopped they threw stones into the water, seeing who could make the biggest splash.

In no time at àll, it seemed, they came to the place where the massive, ominous shadow of the viaduct fell across the dene and the river flowing through it, and there they stared up in awe at the giant arched structure of brick and concrete that bore upon its back one hundred yards of the twin tracks that formed the coastal railway. Shuddering mightily whenever a train roared overhead, the man-made bridge was a never-ending source of amazement and wonder to them . . . And a challenge, too.

It was as they were standing on the bank of the slow-moving river, perhaps fifty feet wide at this point, that they spotted on the opposite bank the local village idiot, 'Wiley Smiley'. Now of course, that was not this unfortunate youth's real name; he was Miles Bellamy, victim of cruel genetic fates since the ill-omened day of his birth some nineteen years earlier. But everyone called him Wiley Smiley.

He was fishing, in a river that had supported nothing bigger than a minnow for many years, with a length of string and a bent pin. He looked up and grinned vacuously as John threw a stone into the water to attract his attention. The stone went quite close to the mark, splashing water over the unkempt youth where he stood a little way out from the far bank, balanced none too securely on slippery rocks. His vacant grin immediately slipped from his face; he became angry, gesturing awkwardly and mouthing incoherently.

'He'll come after us,' said David to his brash companion, his voice just a trifle alarmed.

'No he won't, stupid,' John casually answered, picking up a second, larger stone. 'He can't get across, can he.' It was a statement, not a question, and it was a fact. Here the river was deeper, overflowing from a large pool directly beneath the viaduct which, in the months ahead, children and adults alike would swim in during the hot weekends of summer.

John threw his second missile, deliberately aiming it at the water as close to the enraged idiot as he could without actually hitting him, shouting: 'Yah! Wiley Smiley! Trying to catch a whale, are you?'

Wiley Smiley began to shriek hysterically as the stone splashed down immediately in front of him and a fountain of water geysered over his trousers. Threatening though they now were, his angry caperings upon the rocks looked very funny to the boys (particularly since his rage was impotent), and John began to laugh loud and jeeringly. David, not a cruel boy by nature, found his friend's laughter so infectious that in a few seconds he joined in, adding his own voice to the hilarity.

Then John stooped yet again, straightening up this time with two stones, one of which he offered to his slightly younger companion. Carried completely away now, David accepted the stone and together they hurled their missiles, dancing and laughing until tears rolled down their cheeks as Wiley Smiley received a further dousing. By that time the rocks upon which their victim stood were thoroughly wet and slippery, so that suddenly he lost his balance and sat down backwards into the shallow water.

Climbing clumsily, soggily to his feet, he was greeted by howls of laughter from across the river, which drove him to further excesses of rage. His was a passion which might only find outlet in direct retaliation, revenge. He took a few paces forward, until the water swirled about his knees, then stooped and plunged his arms into the river. There were stones galore beneath the water, and the face of the tormented youth was twisted with hate and fury now as he straightened up and brandished two which were large and jagged.

Where his understanding was painfully slow, Wiley Smiley's strength was prodigious. Had his first stone hit John on the head it might easily have killed him. As it was, the boy ducked at the last moment and the missile flew harmlessly above him. David, too, had to jump to avoid being hurt by a flying rock, and no sooner had the idiot loosed both his stones than he stooped down again to grope in the water for more.

Wiley Smiley's aim was too good for the boys, and his continuing rage was making them begin to feel uncomfortable, so they beat a hasty retreat up the steeply-wooded slope of the dene and made for the walkway that was fastened and ran parallel to the nearside wall of the viaduct. Soon they had climbed out of sight of the poor soul below, but they could still hear his meaningless squawking and shrieking.

A few minutes more of puffing and panting, climbing steeply through trees and saplings, brought them up above the wood and to the edge of a grassy slope. Another hundred yards and they could go over a fence and onto the viaduct. Though no word had passed between them on the subject, it was inevitable that they should end up on the viaduct, one of the most fascinating places in their entire world . . .

The massive structure had been built when first the collieries of the north-east opened up, long before plans were drawn up for the major coast road, and now it linked twin colliery villages that lay opposite each other across the narrow river valley it spanned. Originally constructed solely to accommodate the railway, and used to that end to this very day, with the addition of a walkway, it also provided miners who lived in one village but worked in the other with a shortcut to their respective coal-mines.

While the viaduct itself was of sturdy brick, designed to withstand decade after decade of the heavy traffic that rumbled and clattered across its triple-arched back, the walkway was a comparatively fragile affair. That is not to say that it was not safe, but there were certain dangers and notices had been posted at its approaches to warn users of the presence of at least an element of risk.

Supported upon curving metal arms – iron bars about one and one-half inches in diameter which, springing from the brick and mortar of the viaduct wall, were set perhaps twenty inches apart – the walkway itself was of wooden planks protected by a fence five feet high. There were, however, small gaps where rotten planks had been removed and never replaced, but the miners who used the viaduct were careful and knew the walkway's dangers intimately. All in all the walkway served a purpose and was reasonably safe; one might jump from it, certainly, but only a very careless person or an outright fool would fall. Still, it was no place for anyone suffering from vertigo . . .

Now, as they climbed the fence to stand gazing up at those ribs of iron with their burden of planking and railings, the two boys felt a strange, headlong rushing emotion within them. For this day, of course, was *the* day!

It had been coming for almost a year, since the time when John had stood right where he stood now to boast: 'One day I'll swing hand over hand along those rungs, all the way across. Just like Tarzan.' Yes, they had sensed this day's approach, almost as they might sense Christmas or the end of long, idyllic summer holidays . . . or a visit to the dentist. Something far away, which would eventually arrive, but not yet.

Except that now it had arrived.

'One hundred and sixty rungs,' John breathed, his voice a little fluttery, feeling his palms beginning to itch. 'Yesterday, in the playground, we both did twenty more than that on the climbing-frame.'

'The climbing-frame,' answered David, with a naïve insight and vision far ahead of his age, 'is only seven feet high. The viaduct is about a hundred and fifty.'

John stared at his friend for a second and his eyes narrowed. Suddenly he sneered. 'I might have known it – you're scared, aren't you?'

'No,' David shook his head, lying, 'but it'll soon be lunch-time, and –'

'You *are* scared!' John repeated. 'Like a little kid. We've been practising for months for this, every day of school on the climbing-frame, and now we're ready. You know we can do it.' His tone grew more gentle, urging: 'Look, it's not as if we can't stop if we want to, is it? There's them holes in the fence, and those big gaps in the planks.'

'The first gap,' David answered, noticing how very far away and faint his own voice sounded, 'is almost a third of the way across . . .'

'That's right,' John agreed, nodding his head eagerly. 'We've counted the rungs, haven't we? Just fifty of them to that first wide gap. If we're too tired to go on when we get there, we can just climb up through the gap onto the walkway.'

David, whose face had been turned towards the ground, looked up. He looked straight into his friend's eyes, not at the viaduct, in whose shade they stood. He shivered, but not because he was cold.

John stared right back at him, steadily, encouragingly, knowing that his smaller friend looked for his approval, his reassurance. And he was right, for despite the fact that their ages were very close, David held him up as some sort of hero. No dare-devil, David, but he desperately wished he could be. And now . . . here was his chance.

He simply nodded – then laughed out loud as John gave a wild whoop and shook his young fists at the viaduct. 'Today we'll beat you!' he yelled, then turned and clambered furiously up the last few yards of steep grassy slope to where the first rung might easily be reached with an upward spring. David followed him after a moment's pause, but not before he heard the first arch of the viaduct throw back the challenge in a faintly ringing, sardonic echo of John's cry: 'Beat you . . . beat you . . . beat you . . .'

As he caught up with his ebullient friend, David finally allowed his eyes to glance upward at those skeletal ribs of iron above him. They looked solid, were solid, he knew – but the air beneath them was very thin indeed. John turned to him, his face flushed with excitement. 'You first,' he said.

'Me?' David blanched. 'But –'

'You'll be up onto the walkway first if we get tired,' John pointed out. 'Besides, I go faster than you – and you wouldn't want to be left behind, would you?'

David shook his head. 'No,' he slowly answered, 'I wouldn't want to be left behind.' Then his voice took on an anxious note: 'But you won't hurry me, will you?'

' 'Course not,' John answered. 'We'll just take it nice and easy, like we do at school.'

Without another word, but with his ears ringing strangely and his breath already coming faster, David jumped up and caught hold of the first rung. He swung forward, first one hand to the rung in front, then the other, and so on. He heard John grunt as he too jumped and caught the first rung, and then he gave all his concentration to what he was doing.

Hand over hand, rung by rung, they made their way out over the abyss. Below them the ground fell sharply away, each swing of their arms adding almost two feet to their height, seeming to add tangibly to their weight. Now they were silent, except for an occasional grunt, saving both breath and strength as they worked their way along the underside of the walkway. There was only the breeze that whispered in their ears and the infrequent toot of a motor's horn on the distant road.

As the bricks of the wall moved slowly by, so the distance between rungs seemed to increase, and already David's arms felt tired. He knew that John, too, must be feeling it, for while his friend was bigger and a little stronger, he was also heavier. And sure enough, at a distance of only twenty-five, maybe thirty rungs out towards the centre, John breathlessly called for a rest.

David pulled himself up and hung his arms and his rib-cage over the rung he was on – just as they had practised in the playground – getting comfortable before carefully turning his head to look back. He was shocked to see that John's face was paler than he'd ever known it, that his eyes were staring. When John saw David's doubt, however, he managed a weak grin.

'It's okay,' he said. 'I was – I was just a bit worried about you, that's all. Thought your arms might be getting a bit tired. Have you – have you looked down yet?'

'No,' David answered, his voice mouse-like. *No*, he said again, this time to himself, *and I'm not going to!* He carefully turned his head back to look ahead, where the diminishing line of rungs seemed to stretch out almost infinitely to the far side of the viaduct.

John had been worried about him. Yes, of course he had; that was why his face had looked so funny, so – shrunken. John thought he was frightened, was worried about his self-control, his ability to carry on. Well, David told himself, he had every right to worry; but all the same he felt ashamed that his weakness was so obvious. Even in a position like that, perched so perilously, David's mind was far more concerned with the other boy's opinion of him than with thoughts of possible disaster. And it never once dawned on him, not for a moment, that John might really only be worried about himself . . .

Almost as if to confirm beyond a doubt the fact that John

had little faith in his strength, his courage – as David hung there, breathing deeply, preparing himself for the next stage of the venture – his friend's voice, displaying an unmistakable quaver, came to him again from behind:

'Just another twenty rungs, that's all, then you'll be able to climb up onto the walkway.'

Yes, David thought, *I'll be able to climb up. But then I'll know that I'll never be like you – that you'll always be better than me – because you'll carry on all the way across!* He set his teeth and dismissed the thought. It wasn't going to be like that, he told himself, not this time. After all, it was no different up here from in the playground. You were only higher, that was all. The trick was in not looking down –

As if obeying some unheard command, seemingly with a morbid curiosity of their own, David's eyes slowly began to turn downward, defying him. Their motion was only arrested when David's attention suddenly centred upon a spider-like dot that emerged suddenly from the cover of the trees, scampering frantically up the opposite slope of the valley. He recognised the figure immediately from the faded blue shirt and black trousers that it wore. It was Wiley Smiley.

As David lowered himself carefully into the hanging position beneath his rung and swung forward, he said: 'Across the valley, there – that's Wiley Smiley. I wonder why he's in such a hurry?' There had been something terribly *urgent* about the idiot's quick movements, as if some rare incentive powered them.

'I see him,' said John, sounding more composed now. 'Huh! He's just an old nutter. My dad says he'll do something one of these days and have to be taken away.'

'Do something?' David queried, pausing briefly between swings. An uneasiness completely divorced from the perilous game they were playing rose churningly in his stomach and mind. 'What kind of thing?'

'Dunno,' John grunted. 'But anyway, don't – *uh!* – talk.'

It was good advice: don't talk, conserve wind, strength, take it easy. And yet David suddenly found himself moving faster, dangerously fast, and his fingers were none too sure as they moved from one rung to the next. More than once he was hanging by one hand while the other groped blindly for support.

It was very, very important now to close the distance between himself and the sanctuary of the gap in the planking. True, he had made up his mind just a few moments ago to carry on beyond that gap – as far as he could go before admitting defeat, submitting – but all such resolutions were gone now as quickly as they came. His one thought was of climbing up to safety.

It had something to do with Wiley Smiley and the eager, *determined* way he had been scampering up the far slope. Towards the viaduct. Something to do with that, yes, and with what John had said about Wiley Smiley being taken away one day ... for *doing* something. David's mind dared not voice its fears too specifically, not even to itself ...

Now, except for the occasional grunt – that and the private pounding of blood in their ears – the two boys were silent, and only a minute or so later David saw the gap in the planking. He had been searching for it, sweeping the rough wood of the planks stretching away overhead anxiously until he saw the wide, straight crack that quickly enlarged as he swung closer. Two planks were missing here, he knew, just sufficient to allow a boy to squirm through the gap without too much trouble.

His breath coming in sobbing, glad gasps, David was just a few rungs away from safety when he felt the first tremors vibrating through the great structure of the viaduct. It was like the trembling of a palsied giant. 'What's that?' he cried out loud, terrified, clinging desperately to the rung above his head.

'It's a – *uh!* – train!' John gasped, his own voice now very hoarse and plainly frightened. 'We'll have to – *uh!* – wait until it's gone over.'

Quickly, before the approaching train's vibrations could

shake them loose, the boys hauled themselves up into positions of relative safety and comfort, perching on their rungs beneath the planks of the walkway. There they waited and shivered in the shadow of the viaduct, while the shuddering rumble of the train drew ever closer, until, in a protracted clattering of wheels on rails, the monster rushed by unseen overhead. The trembling quickly subsided and the train's distant whistle proclaimed its derision; it was finished with them.

Without a word, holding back a sob that threatened to develop into full-scale hysteria, David lowered himself once more into the full-length hanging position; behind him, breathing harshly and with just the hint of a whimper escaping from his lips, John did the same. Two, three more forward swings and the gap was directly overhead. David looked up, straight up to the clear sky.

'Hurry!' said John, his voice the tiniest whisper. 'My hands are starting to feel funny . . .'

David pulled himself up and balanced across his rung, tremulously took away one hand and grasped the edge of the wooden planking. Pushing down on the hand that grasped the rung and hauling himself up with the other, finally he knelt on the rung and his head emerged through the gap in the planks. He looked along the walkway . . .

. . . There, not three feet away, legs widespread and eyes burning with a fanatical hatred, crouched Wiley Smiley. David saw him, saw the pointed stick he held, felt a thrill of purest horror course through him. Then, in the next instant, the idiot lunged forward and his mouth opened in a demented parody of a laugh. David saw the lightning movement of the sharpened stick and tried to avoid its thrust. He felt the point strike his forehead just above his left eye and fell back, off balance, arms flailing. Briefly his left hand made contact with the planking again, then lost it, and he fell with a shriek . . . across the rung that lay directly beneath him. It was not a long fall but fear and panic had already winded David; he simply closed his eyes and sobbed, hanging on for dear life, motionless. But only for a handful of seconds.

Warm blood trickled from David's forehead, falling on his hands where he gripped the rung. Something was prodding the back of his neck, jabbing viciously. The pain brought him back from the abyss and he opened his eyes to risk one sharp, fearful glance upwards. Wiley Smiley was kneeling at the edge of the gap, his stick already moving downward for another jab. Again David moved his head to avoid the thrust of the stick, and once more the point scraped his forehead.

Behind him David could hear John moaning and screaming alternately: 'Oh, Mum! Dad! It's Wiley Smiley! It's him, him, *him!* He'll kill us, kill us . . .' Galvanised into action, David lowered himself for the third time into the hanging position and swung forward, away from the inflamed idiot's deadly stick. Two rungs, three, then he carefully turned about face and hauled himself up to rest. He looked at John through the blood that dripped slowly into one eye, blurring his vision.

David blinked to clear his eye of blood, then said: 'John, you'll have to turn round and go back, get help. He's got me here. I can't go forward any further, I don't think, and I can't come back. I'm stuck. But it's only fifty rungs back to the start. You can do it easy, and if you get tired you can always rest. I'll wait here until you fetch help.'

'Can't, can't, *can't*,' John babbled, trembling wildly where he lay half across his rung. Tears ran down the older boy's cheeks and fell into space like salty rain. He was deathly white, eyes staring, frozen. Suddenly yellow urine flooded from the leg of his short trousers in a long burst. When he saw this, David, too, wet himself, feeling the burning of his water against his legs but not caring. He felt very tiny, very weak now, and he knew that fear and shock were combining to exhaust him.

Then, as a silhouette glimpsed briefly in a flash of lightning, David saw in his mind's eye a means of salvation. 'John,' he urgently called out to the other boy. 'Do you remember near the middle of the viaduct? There are two gaps close together in the walkway, maybe only a dozen or so rungs apart.'

Almost imperceptibly, John nodded, never once moving his frozen eyes from David's face. 'Well,' the younger boy continued, barely managing to keep the hysteria out of his own voice, 'if we can swing to –' Suddenly David's words were cut off by a burst of insane laughter from above, followed immediately by a loud, staccato thumping on the boards as Wiley Smiley leapt crazily up and down.

'No, no, *no* –' John finally cried out in answer to David's proposal. His paralysis broken, he began to sob unashamedly. Then, shaking his head violently, he said: 'I can't move – can't move!' His voice became the merest whisper. 'Oh, God – Mum – Dad! I'll fall, I'll fall!'

'You won't fall, you git – *coward*!' David shouted. Then his jaw fell open in a gasp. John, a coward! But the other boy didn't even seem to have heard him. Now he was trembling as wildly as before and his eyes were squeezed tight shut.

'Listen,' David said. 'If you don't come . . . then I'll leave you. You wouldn't want to be left on your own, would you?' It was an echo as of something said a million years ago.

John stopped sobbing and opened his eyes. They opened very wide, unbelieving. 'Leave me?'

'Listen,' David said again. 'The next gap is only about twenty rungs away, and the one after that is only another eight or nine more. Wiley Smiley can't get after both of us at once, can he?'

'You go,' said John, his voice taking on fresh hope and his eyes blinking rapidly. 'You go and maybe he'll follow you. Then I'll climb up and – and chase him off . . .'

'You won't be able to chase him off,' said David scornfully, 'not just you on your own. You're not big enough.'

'Then I'll . . . I'll run and fetch help.'

'What if he doesn't follow after me?' David asked. 'If we both go, he's bound to follow us.'

'David,' John said, after a moment or two. 'David, I'm . . . frightened.'

'You'll have to be quick across the gap,' David said, ignoring John's last statement. 'He's got that stick – and of course he'll be listening to us.'

'I'm frightened,' John whispered again.

David nodded. 'Okay, you stay where you are, if that's what you want – but I'm going on.'

'Don't leave me, don't leave me!' John cried out, his shriek accompanied by a peal of mad and bubbling laughter from the unseen idiot above. 'Don't go!'

'I have to, or we're both finished,' David answered. He slid down into the hanging position and turned about face, noting as he did so that John was making to follow him, albeit in a dangerous, panicky fashion. 'Wait to see if Wiley Smiley follows me!' he called back over his shoulder.

'No. I'm coming, I'm coming!'

From far down below in the valley David heard a horrified shout, then another. They had been spotted. Wiley Smiley heard the shouting, too, and his distraction was sufficient to allow John to pass by beneath him unhindered. From above, the two boys now heard the idiot's worried mutterings and gruntings, and the hesitant sound of his feet as he slowly kept pace with them along the walkway. He could see them through the narrow cracks between the planks, but the cracks weren't wide enough for him to use his stick.

David's arms and hands were terribly numb and aching by the time he reached the second gap, but seeing the gloating, twisted features of Wiley Smiley leering down at him he ducked his head and swung on to where he was once more protected by the planks above him. John had stopped short of the second gap, hauling himself up into the safer, resting position.

Above them Wiley Smiley was mewling viciously like a wild animal, howling as if in torment. He rushed crazily back and forth from gap to gap, jabbing uselessly at the empty air between the vacant rungs. The boys could see the bloodied point of the stick striking down first through one open space, then the other. David achingly waited until he saw the stick appear at the gap in front of him and then, when it retreated and he heard Wiley Smiley's footsteps hurrying overhead, swung swiftly across to the other side. There he turned about to face John, and with what felt like his last ounce of strength pulled himself up to rest.

Now, for the first time, David dared to look down. Below, running up the riverbank and waving frantically, were the ant-like figures of three men. They must have been out for a Saturday morning stroll when they'd spotted the two boys hanging beneath the viaduct's walkway. One of them stopped running and put his hands up to his mouth. His shout floated up to the boys on the clear air: 'Hang on, lads, hang on!'

'Help!' David and John cried out together, as loud as they could. 'Help! – Help!'

'We're coming, lads,' came the answering shout. The men hurriedly began to climb the wooded slope on their side of the river and disappeared into the trees.

'They'll be here soon,' David said, wondering if it would be soon enough. His whole body ached and he felt desperately weak and sick.

'Hear that, Wiley Smiley?' John cried hysterically, staring up at the boards above him. 'They'll be here soon – and then you'll be taken away and locked up!' There was no answer. A slight wind had come up off the sea and was carrying a salty tang to them where they lay across their rungs.

'They'll take you away and lock you up,' John cried again, the ghost of a sob in his voice; but once more the only answer was the slight moaning of the wind. John looked across at David, maybe twenty-five feet away, and said: 'I think . . . I think he's gone.' Then he gave a wild shout. 'He's gone. *He's gone!*'

'I didn't hear him go,' said David, dubiously.

John was very much more his old self now. 'Oh, he's gone, all right. He saw those men coming and cleared off. David, I'm going up!'

'You'd better wait,' David cried out as his friend slid down to hang at arm's length from his rung. John ignored the advice; he swung forward hand over hand until he was under the far gap in the planking. With a grunt of exertion, he forced the tired muscles of his arms to pull his tired body up. He got his rib-cage over the rung, flung a hand up and took hold of the naked plank to one side of the gap, then –

In that same instant David sensed rather than heard the furtive movement overhead. 'John!' he yelled. 'He's still there – *Wiley Smiley's still there!*'

But John had already seen Wiley Smiley; the idiot had made his presence all too plain, and already his victim was screaming. The boy fell back fully into David's view, the hand he had thrown up to grip the edge of the plank returning automatically to the rung, his arms taking the full weight of his falling body, somehow sustaining him. There was a long gash in his cheek from which blood freely flowed.

'Move forward!' David yelled, terror pulling his lips back in a snarling mask. 'Forward, where he can't get at you . . .'

John heard him and must have seen in some dim, frightened recess of his mind the commonsense of David's advice. Panting hoarsely – partly in dreadful fear, partly from hideous emotional exhaustion – he swung one hand forward and caught at the next rung. And at that precise moment, in the split second while John hung suspended between the two rungs with his face turned partly upward, Wiley Smiley struck again.

David was witness to it all. He heard the maniac's rising, gibbering shriek of triumph as the sharp point of the stick lanced unerringly down, and John's answering cry of purest agony as his left eye flopped bloodily out onto his cheek, lying there on a white thread of nerve and gristle. He saw John clap *both hands* to his monstrously altered face, and watched in starkest horror as his friend seemed to stand for a moment, defying gravity, on the thin air. Then John was gone, dwindling away down a drafty funnel of air, while rising came the piping, diminishing scream that would haunt David until his dying day, a scream that was cut short after what seemed an impossibly long time.

John had fallen. At first David couldn't accept it, but then it began to sink in. His friend had fallen. He moaned and shut his eyes tightly, lying half across and clinging to his rung so fiercely that he could no longer really feel his bloodless fingers at all. John had fallen . . .

Then – perhaps it was only a minute or so later, perhaps an hour, David didn't know – there broke in on his perceptions the sound of clumping, hurrying feet on the boards above, and a renewed, even more frenzied attack of gibbering and shrieking from Wiley Smiley. David forced his eyes open as the footsteps came to a halt directly overhead. He heard a gruff voice:

'Jim, you keep that bloody – *Thing* – away, will you? He's already killed one boy today. Frank, give us a hand here.'

A face, inverted, appeared through the hole in the planks not three feet away from David's own face. The mouth opened and the same voice, but no longer gruff, said: 'It's okay now, son. Everything's okay. Can you move?'

In answer, David could only shake his head negatively. Overtaxed muscles, violated nerves had finally given in. He was frozen on his perch; he would stay where he was now until he was either taken off physically or until he fainted.

Dimly the boy heard the voice again, and others raised in an urgent hubbub, but he was too far gone to make out any words that were said. He was barely aware that the face had been withdrawn. A few seconds later there came a banging and tearing from immediately above him; a small shower of tiny pieces of wood, dust, and homogenous débris fell upon his head and shoulders. Then daylight flooded down to illuminate more brightly the shaded area beneath the walkway. Another board was torn away, and another.

The inverted face again appeared, this time at the freshly-made opening, and an exploratory hand reached down. Using its kindly voice, the face said: 'Okay, son, we'll have you out of there in a jiffy. I – *uh!* – can't quite seem to reach you, but it's only a matter of a few inches. Do you think you can –'

The voice was cut off by a further outburst of incoherent shrieking and jabbering from Wiley Smiley. The face and hand withdrew momentarily and David heard the voice yet again. This time it was angry. 'Look, see if you can keep that damned idiot back, will you? And keep him quiet, for God's sake!'

The hand came back, large and strong, reaching down. David still clung with all his remaining strength to the rung, and though he knew what was expected of him – what he must do to win himself the prize of continued life – all sense of feeling had quite gone from his limbs and even shifting his position was a very doubtful business.

'Boy,' said the voice, as the hand crept inches closer and the inverted face stared into his, 'if you could just reach up your hand, I –'

'I'll – I'll try to do it,' David whispered.

'Good, good,' his would-be rescuer calmly, quietly answered. 'That's it, lad, just a few inches. Keep your balance, now.'

David's hand crept up from the rung and his head, neck, and shoulder slowly turned to allow it free passage. Up it tremblingly went, reaching to meet the hand stretching down from above. The boy and the man, each peered into the other's straining face, and an instant later their fingertips touched –

There came a mad shriek, a frantic pounding of feet and cries of horror and wild consternation from above. The inverted face went white in a moment and disappeared, apparently dragged backwards. The hand disappeared, too. And that was the very moment that David had chosen to free himself of the rung and give himself into the protection of his rescuer . . .

He flailed his arms in a vain attempt to regain his balance. Numb, cramped, cold with that singular icy chill experienced only at death's positive approach, his limbs would not obey. He rolled forward over the bar and his legs were no longer strong enough to hold him. He didn't even feel the toes of his shoes as they struck the rung – the last of him to have contact with the viaduct – before his fall began. And if the boy thought anything at all during that fall, well, those thoughts will never be known. Later he could not remember.

Oh, there was to be a later, but David could hardly have believed it while he was falling. And yet he was not unconscious. There were vague impressions: of the sky, the looming arch of the viaduct flying past, trees below, the sea on the horizon, then the sky again, all slowly turning. There was a composite whistling, of air displaced and air ejected from lungs contracted in a high-pitched scream. And then, it seemed a long time later, there was the impact . . .

But David did not strike the ground . . . he struck the pool. The deep swimming hole. The blessed, merciful river!

He had curled into a ball – the foetal position, almost – and this doubtless saved him. His tightly-curled body entered the water with very little injury, however much of a splash it caused. Deep as the water was, nevertheless David struck the bottom with force, the pain and shock awakening whatever facilities remained functional in the motor areas of his brain. Aided by his resultant struggling, however weak, the ballooning air in his clothes bore him surely to the surface. The river carried him a few yards downstream to where the banks formed a bottleneck for the pool.

Through all the pain David felt his knees scrape pebbles, felt his hands on the mud of the bank, and where willpower presumably was lacking, instinct took over. Somehow he crawled from the pool, and somehow he hung on grimly to consciousness. Away from the water, still he kept on crawling, as from the horror of his experience. Unseeing, he moved towards the towering unconquered colossus of the viaduct. He was quite blind as of yet, there was only a red, impenetrable haze before his bloodied eyes; he heard nothing but a sick roaring in his head. Finally his shoulder struck the bole of a tree that stood in the shelter of the looming brick giant, and there he stopped crawling, propped against the tree.

Slowly, very slowly the roaring went out of his ears, the red haze before his eyes was replaced by lightning flashes and kaleidoscopic shapes and colours. Normal sound suddenly returned with a great pain in his ears. A rush of wind rustled the leaves of the trees, snatching away and then giving back a distant shouting which seemed to have its source overhead. Encased in his shell of pain, David did not immediately relate the shouting to his miraculous escape. Sight returned a few moments later and he began to cry wrackingly with relief; he had thought himself permanently blind. And perhaps even now he had not been completely wrong, for his eyes had plainly been knocked out of order. Something was – *must* be – desperately wrong with them.

David tried to shake his head to clear it, but this action only brought fresh, blinding pain. When the nausea subsided he blinked his eyes, clearing them of blood and peering bewilderedly about at his surroundings. It was as he had suspected: the colours were all wrong. No, he blinked again, some of them seemed perfectly normal.

For instance: the bark of the tree against which he leaned was brown enough, and its dangling leaves were a fresh green. The sky above was blue, reflected in the river, and the bricks of the viaduct were a dull orange. Why then was the grass beneath him a lush red streaked with yellow and grey? Why was this unnatural grass wet and sticky, and –

– And why were these tatters of dimly familiar clothing flung about in exploded, scarlet disorder?

When his reeling brain at last delivered the answer, David opened his mouth to scream, fainting before he could do so. He fell face down into the sticky embrace of his late friend.

Fog In My Throat

by

R. A. LAFFERTY

Raphael Aloysius Lafferty (1915–) and his work are impossible to summarise here. He lives in Tulsa, Oklahoma. For most of his life he worked as an electrical engineer, for jobbers; now he writes full-time. His extraordinary books include Past Master, The Reefs Of Earth, Fourth Mansions, Arrive At Easterwine, *and the collection* Nine Hundred Grandmothers. *His short story 'Eurema's Dam' won a Hugo Award; he has been several times short-listed for Nebula Awards by the Science Fiction Writers of America, and nominated for Hugos.*

Interviewed in The Alien Critic, *Lafferty tells how the 'disorders' of his personality are tied together by his Catholicism: 'the inescapable logic, the complete clarity . . . however much I stumble and fall short of it, I know it is there and what it is.' There is apparent disorder in his work, but look again: he juggles the products of his wild imagination with great skill – his inimitable style unites them. Thus, despite what looks at first like zany humour, this story is dreadfully terrifying.*

I will show you fear in a handful of dust.
          The Waste Land, Eliot.

Fear death? – to feel the fog in my throat,
The mist in my face.
          Prospice, Browning.

'I have never known a person who feared death when he finally came to it,' Cornelius Rudisijl said. This Rudy was a vital old man of overflowing facilities. By the year count he shouldn't have been too far from death, or at least from the thought of it: but it would be hard to imagine him afraid of that terminator or of anything else.

'I'm afraid of death,' said Gretchen Schrik with a shudder. 'There's no denying it. It's my strongest obsession, this fear.'

'And you're twenty years old,' Rudisijl said, 'and probably seventy years away from death. You will not be afraid of it when it comes. Nobody ever is. And that's the mystery of it.'

The strong, sad, and sonorous 'Song of Job' was heard in the near distance. Job was one of the clinic rats who had received a certain specific, but Job had been an accident-prone rat before that. Now he played his strange and agonising music on the glass harp and he also raised his voice in his despairful song.

'What if I should die suddenly?' Gretchen shivered. 'What if I should die today? Even the talk of it scares me.'

'Well, what if death does come to you today?' Rudisijl asked. 'I tell you that you will not be afraid of it when it comes.'

Jubilee and Halleluiah, two other clinic rats who had received the specific, were raising their voices and their instruments in songs somewhat more hopeful than the 'Song of Job', but nevertheless they were very intricate songs, for rats at least.

'Gretchen is afraid of death,' Rita Malley said in friendly mockery. 'And my own consultant tells me that I'm afraid of life.'

Three and a half miles away, across town, another comparatively young person was worrying about death. He also was near twenty years of age and had a normal expectancy of another seventy years of life. A normal expectancy, but the life that he lived wasn't normal. An actuary wouldn't have given him seventy more years: probably not five years unless he changed his ways.

The young man's name was Lucius Flammus and he was lean and mean. He was a legend among the young and sudden and passioned people. He was their duke; he was their flame. Sometimes they called him the Angel of Death. He was involved with death often and he feared it pathologically. This Flammus was going over his long hand-guns with care and intensity. The guns were like other souls to him and he would not neglect them. He had the feel of tall excitement whenever he touched them.

'I will kill a man today,' Flammus said, and this statement of his always marked a high of pleasure-pain in anticipation. 'And he will die in terror, in total terror. This is the special part, the part that hasn't happened before. Ah, this will be the greatest one ever! Or the first of my great ones.'

Then Flammus' premonition and excitement clarified itself a little bit.

'There is more to it,' he barked in sharp excitement. 'There is bonus after bonus. I will kill a young woman today for an even sharper scene. Aw, but she will not die in terror. I wonder why she won't.'

Flammus sometimes said that he wasn't a killer by choice. But sometimes he deceived himself and sometimes he lied. And also these things happened regularly in his trade, and he took what satisfaction he could from them. His satisfaction from killing, however, was always encased in a separate horror and fear of his own:

'What if I also am killed today?'

'I will tell you something else,' Dr Cornelius Rudisijl was saying back at the Advanced Experimental Clinic. 'In the seventy years that I have been in the flesh and blood trade, I have seen one hundred thousand people die, or seen them shortly after death. One third of them had died violently, many of them cut off in their primes or youths or even childhoods. I have seen none of them who was afraid of death at the very last minute, and I have never seen even a hint of fear or horror on any dead face.

'I have seen persons who were drowned, who were burned to death, who were done in by knife torture in internecine squabbles, who have died in quicksand over their heads. I have seen three who were sliced in half by sharks. I have seen the face of a man who was pinned down by one rockfall and then killed by a second rockfall which he had to see coming down on him. I have seen the faces of steel-workers who fell to their deaths from high buildings and high bridges and who lived the long conscious seconds during their falls. I have seen the faces of sky-guys and stunters whose parachutes failed to open. I have seen the face of a man caught and eaten, from the feet up, by a crocodile. I have seen many thousands of persons die in pain, and others die without the distraction of pain; and none of them died in fear. I have had persons tell me, some time before their deaths, that they were hysterical with the fear of dying. And yet they died serene. Everybody dies serene. That's a final blessing that makes up for a lot.'

'I simply do not believe that, Rudy,' said Fred Renier who was another of the high doctors at the clinic. 'I've surely seen half as many people dying and dead as you have. I cannot, right now, remember one who died in outright terror, but others have seen terror deaths, and the cameras record many of them. I remember one prize-winning photograph of the year past. It still haunts me sometimes. There was –'

'There have been many such photographs,' Rudisijl said, 'and there is only one thing wrong with them. All such pictures were taken too soon. None of them was taken at the absolute moment of death. There was one case a few months back, and it may be the case that you refer to, of a jumping suicide. The picture was taken just as he cleared his ledge on his downward leap to the predictable and stereotyped 'Jump! Jump! Jump!' shouts of the happy people below. Yes, the face, as shown in that prize-winning photograph taken by that journalistic photographer as he crept along the ledge to get the best shot, that face did show absolute horror and bottomless fear. But I saw the shattered man after he was laid out. His head and face were broken, as was the rest of him, but the expression on his face was whole. Believe me, it was the expression of serenity. A change had come over that man during his four hundred foot plunge downward, a beneficent change.'

Now there was heard the rhythmic chorus of guinea pigs singing. The guineas are normally almost soundless. They do not sing at all in the ordinary course of things, and who ever heard of them singing in chorus? But these guinea pigs had received the specific.

'Believe me, I wouldn't hit the street with a serene expression after such a leap,' said Rita Malley who was a young lady doctor there. 'I fear death as much as Gretchen does, and I bet I can scream louder. There would have been screaming horror on my face.'

'No, there would not,' Rudisijl insisted. 'Sometimes the period seems a little short for what must be a chemical reaction to take place, but it *does* take place no matter how short the time. I've known it to be within fractions of a second. And what we are working on here at the clinic is something akin to this serenity-in-death reaction. We have come up with the serenity-in-everything specific. Whether it will be required to work in fractions of a second I don't know, but that is possible. We are looking for the specific against all anxiety, against all worry, against all unhappiness, against all frustration. I said long ago that if the specific for all these things was in the zoochemical field that we would find it. Now the three of you confirm it to me that we probably *have* found the specific.'

'Oh happy rats!' Gretchen Schrik cried. 'By all our happy creatures, I'm sure that we've found it.'

It really seemed as if they had found the specific. They had created new races of happy rats, of unfrustrated rats, of outright delightful rats, of responsible rats, of intelligent rats.

'And of noble rats,' Gretchen said, 'and of thoughtful rats.

Yes, I mean it, thoughtful rats, devoted rats, rats that are aware of something very great. These are rats that will not waste their time with small worries.'

And such races of guinea pigs also had been brought about, and promising races of several other creatures.

The specific that was being used on these creatures had the simplicity and symmetry of concept that all great specifics possess. It was an electrostatic-condition parahormone that swam in globules of neuroendocrine substance. It was needled into the two main arteries leading into the brain. It worked quickly. It made happy and superior creatures, and it kept them superior.

With one exception, that only Gretchen knew about. She discovered a specific-treated rat that had died, not from anything connected with the specific, but from simple rat scours. The scours is a rapid wasting disease but it is not painful. And yet the dead rat was contorted and deformed with a look of total horror. Gretchen destroyed the beastie without saying anything to anyone. It was too akin to her in its dying fear. She thought that perhaps she was mistaken, that such an expression in a rat hadn't the same meaning as such an expression in a person. But Gretchen had close feeling for the rats, and deep down she knew that it had died in real horror.

But that was the only rat that died during the weeks of the experiments with the various forms of the specific. All the other animals were not only healthy but they seemed to be fastidiously healthy. It was almost as if they took the greatest care to avoid sickness and death, to avoid any discomforts that might lead to them.

'This will be one of the greatest of all advances,' Rudisijl said. 'I believe that it is mental clarity that the infusions give to the rats. I believe that it is total freedom from superstition. Yes, of course rats are normally subject to superstition. You aren't familiar with Reichard's *Rattenaberglaube und Nagetierpsychologie*? I believe that a cloud, of unknown function, had entered all minds, animal and human. I believe that our specific will shatter that cloud.'

'Maybe there is good reason for the cloud,' Gretchen said. 'Maybe the obstruction was put there for good cause, and its removal will be dangerous.'

'No. There cannot be good reason for such a mind-cloud, for such an obstruction. It is a deception and a darkening, however it happened. Our specific will, among so many other things, will bring an end to such deceptions and concealments. It will bring the beginning of total clarity.'

'Maybe it is possible for clarity to be too total,' Gretchen said.

'I don't think so,' Rudisijl told them. 'What are you trying to say, Gretchen? Have your own anxieties and terrors not faded, Gretchen? I believe they have faded just from your observing the removal of so many frustrations and worries in the creatures.'

'Yes, my own anxieties and terrors *have* faded, to a great extent,' Gretchen admitted. 'But I'm not at all sure that final clarity is what I want. I believe that what I want is to be rescued *from* that final clarity.'

Well, Gretchen's anxieties had faded, but they had a long way to fade. Only a month before this she had written a panic-stricken letter to her mother:

'— it is no good dodging it, mama; it is no good running away from it. It will be with me for as long as there is a me. And then this thing (the fear) will still be here when I am gone. It is an independent entity and it does not need a person to attach to. The dreadful fear, the choking fear is itself a being.

'It would be no good me coming home again. Traps are set for me there. I have fled from this terror all my life, and it is waiting for me in a ravening form in every place that I have ever fled. I will not outgrow this. I do not believe that anybody is free from this fear. I don't know why we don't all die from the fear of death. Really, I believe that it *is* what we all die from.

'Oh, there are things to do. And there are lives to be lived, as you say. I know those things and I do those things. I am the most occupied person ever known. But the main thing is always there waiting. Do not any others fear it as much as I do? My psychologist says that he doesn't know about all the others, but *he* fears it as much as I do. He is a very honest man. And the fear of death is all the horrors rolled into one.

'Ghost-fears and night-horrors are parts of it, weak surmises of what may be waiting for us when the lights finally go out. But I am pretty sure that the reality, or the terrible screaming unreality, will be worse than any of our surmises.

'Falling-horror dreams are parts of our death-fear. The hysterical fear of falling does not reside in the threat of crashing at the bottom of the fall: rather it is the dread of *not* coming to a bottom, *ever*.

'Experiences of choking, strangulation, smothering, and drowning are parts of it. It is the suffocating fog in the throat of which the poet wrote. It is the rape of the breath that is the life.

'Buried-alive terrors are part of it. We will be buried, or we will be burned or otherwise destroyed; but do we hope to be dead forever or to be alive again in our burial?

'Form-change horror is part of the death-fear. This is the frightfulness of common persons and creatures turning into monsters and snakes and ravening animals. It is the dread of what we may see when our temporary flesh-masks are gone. And yet all these are the more pleasant of the fearful alternatives: and the least pleasant alternative is to change into nothing.

'Walking corpses make up one precinct of the personal and universal death-horror dream. But even walking corpses are the best of the several choices. And the worst of them is the corpse that will not walk again, not in a million aeons.

'The deprivation of support, especially in the case of small children, the being left alone, is an intrinsic part of it. It is the case of being left alone forever, of going to a place where there are no other places or people, where there have never been others. Death is the longest of all lonelinesses and there is no way that it can be tolerated either in sanity or in madness. It is too extreme to be borne by humans. And is extinction a way of bearing it?

'But extinction is the most horrible thing possible, to my mind. And it appears that it is the most likely of the sequences. Were I given a choice between extinction and hell, and I am not sure that we are not all given that perpetual standing choice as a part of our eternal torture, I would choose hell again and again and again. And I do mean the screaming-pain hell a billion times magnified and continuing for the infinite exponent of forever.

'Ah well, I'm sorry to have this little nervous flare-up. It will pass, of course. It always does. And then it will come back seven times more fierce than it ever was before. It always does. You used to say that I was too serious a child. Well, this is what I have always been serious about. What else in life, besides death, is there to be serious about?

'Everything else going well. Doctor Fred Renier likes me, I think. I can probably land him if I want him. He is rich and successful and a great doctor and a fine man. And he is an ultimate fire-worm like all the rest of us and he will die the wormy death. Why, whenever I begin to like a man, do I see him in his death and corruption?

'The town is lively, the shows here are great, the people are witty and some of them are even friendly, and it has been the most entertaining summer of my life. Almost it distracts me. Mr Rudisijl says that death-fears always diminish and disappear with the closer approach of death itself. How does he know? He has not been there any more than I have. We go, one at a time, bent over and deformed, through that door.

'Your hysterical and loving daughter, Gretchen the wretchen.'

Really Gretchen was a normal and well-balanced young woman who was full of the joy of life. Everybody has a bug or two biting 'em. And Gretchen's bug may have been the most common of them all, that little old death bug so often disguised.

She had an interesting job. She was a degreed doctor while still quite young. She was working at one of the clinics where the greatest breakthroughs ever will be made in just a day or two, or have already been made in fact, and need only a bit more testing before being put into effect. The greatest breakthrough ever was working on the animals, and it would surely work on the people. Why do the animals always get the best of everything first?

And those animals! What do you make of gallant animals? – for that is what they seemed to be. What do you make of guinea pigs and hamsters and rats that acquire a sudden air of responsibility, of fairness, of nobility, of thoughtfulness, of deep seriousness, and this accompanied by the removal of all their little frustrations? Well, what *do* you make of them? It was as if the treated animals were now all possessed of a secret, of a sad secret even, and were resolved to behave all the better for knowing that secret.

There was some argument about the new mental attitude of the laboratory animals that had received the clarifying specific, but nobody argued that they had not become better and more intricate animals with their infusions. Rita Malley (it was she who had made the little glass harps that the animals could play by gnawing on the ends of the glass reeds) was sure that the animals had become more intelligent, and in ways beyond that showed by their improved test scores.

'And the animals are making themselves as agreeable as possible,' Rita said that day. 'I wonder why. They have all picked up the habit of bringing to me, and to you others, too, I'm sure, bright objects that they pick up in their recreation area. They bring these things and they present them as offerings. Really they do! And there's something else that you must have noticed: the appearance of art with them. We will have to devise equipment and means and opportunities to see just how deep this new artistic impulse goes in them. They play the harps and they sing individually and in chorus. They make pictures in their recreation areas out of pebbles and rocks and sticks. They begin to build stepped pyramids out of their play-toy blocks. I'm not sure, but I believe that some of their new scurrying around, and standing still in queer attitudes, and mock fighting, and chittering in a variety of different voices, I believe that this is a form of drama. They're putting on plays, that's what they're doing. Why?'

'For sheer joy, for intense joy,' Doctor Rudisijl said. 'They are completely free of all fears and frustrations now, so they live in an intensity of joy.'

'You're wrong, Rudy,' Doctor Renier said thoughtfully. 'There *is* a fear element in their intensity.'

'There is not,' Rudisijl said. 'And I am never wrong.'

Well, the test animals had entered a period of blooming culture and endeavour, and they all partook thoroughly of it. Except one, except one more.

For Gretchen found one more dead animal, a hamster this time, just before noon that day. It seemed to have died of black-water fever, but that is seldom fatal in a hamster. Whatever it had died of, the body and head and face were contorted by a horror-fear that was really beyond accepting. It had been an insane and killing fear that had put an end to that hamster: the vestiges of black-water fever were only trifles.

But there should have been two dozen of the animals dying of natural causes during the period of the experiments, and there had only been these two. Gretchen destroyed it, and she went to the other people while hesitating as to whether she should tell them about it.

At high noon that day, there was a crash of glass in one of the little meeting rooms of the clinic, and the noonday devil stood in the midst of them holding two smoking long-pistols. The noonday devil was a young man named Lucius Flammus, sometimes called by the sudden people of his crowd the Angel of Death.

He needn't have come crashing through that little glass screen. It was an ornamental thing only. He could have gone around it. And his long-pistols were not smoking from recent use. They were smoking from a piece of dry ice placed, for effect, in the barrel of each of them. But Flammus played the role of some torrid avenger well. He was a striking and menacing appearance there.

'I've come for the big stuff, the heavy stuff, the straight stuff,' this Flammus spat from behind his pistols.

'No, that's not what you've come for,' Rita Malley said, and she was white and shaking with fright. 'Which one of us? Oh, which one of us?' she asked.

'You'll never get away with this, man,' Doctor Renier jibbered out of a terrified mouth.

'Why certainly he'll get away with it,' Doctor Rudisijl said easily. 'We will give him several kilos of the big stuff, and then he will go. It happens every day. It happens at this clinic two or three times a year. Why are you all so terrified?'

Doctor Renier, Gretchen Schrik, and Rita Malley were indeed terrified, hysterically fearful, on the edge of shrieking. And so was Flammus the Death Angel himself. He was gloriously sick with his fear. Even the chorus of singing guinea pigs in the near distance had the welling hopefulness of their paean cut deeply into by a sharp uneasiness rising into a stark fear. And Renier, Gretchen, Rita, and Lucius Flammus were all in the grip of a shaking grey horror.

'What is all the nonsense?' Rudisijl was asking. 'Here! Here's a kilo of it, man. Now be off!' And Rudisijl dropped a packet into the slung shoulder-bag that Flammus wore.

'He did not come for that, Rudy,' Renier spoke in shaking words. 'He came to kill one of us. The big stuff is big to him, but killing is bigger. He is a pathological killer.'

'To kill one of you, yes, that's the big thing,' the insane and terror-shook Flammus hammered out through his chattering teeth. 'Oh, aw, I – forgot. It's to kill two of you this time. I don't know why.'

Rudisijl laughed with sharp contempt. He looked at those four dread-filled faces with mordant humour. 'What difference will it make?' he asked in a hard voice. 'A little trashy event is about to take place. Why try to inflate it into something big? There are no big events.'

The fear and horror went out of Gretchen Schrik's face in a twinkling instant. A calmness and a patient serenity came over her instead. But Rudisijl's superior calm was shattered in the same moment. Shattered by the same moment, likely.

'No, not Gretchen!' he shouted. 'She's better than we knew. Anybody but Gretchen!'

The death-fear had gone out of Gretchen in a second because she was going to die in another second. And death-calm is automatic with all persons.

Rudisijl struck one of the long-pistols from Flammus' hand and sent it clattering to the floor. Flammus shot Gretchen dead with his other pistol. And there was no slight trace of fear on her dead face.

Then Flammus shot Rudisijl who was grappling with him, and the doctor fell heavily to the floor. The death-terror had now gone out of the pathological Flammus as it had gone out of Gretchen. In a second it was replaced by a wooden look without fear, a look of indifferent acceptance, the closest thing to serenity that could happen to someone like Flammus. The death-fear had gone out of him in a second because he was going to die in another second. And nobody ever fears death when he finally comes to it.

Renier had taken Flammus' first pistol from the floor, and he killed him with it.

Doctor Rudisijl was in double-voiced shouting hysteria. In the lower tone he dribbled out fear-jerky explanations as his life flowed away from him in unstaunchable bleeding. And in his high tone, he screamed, uncontrollably and horribly.

44

Doctor Renier had given the specific to Doctor Rudisijl at Rudisijl's own dying request. Rudisijl said that he knew he was dying anyhow and he didn't want to go with his curiosity about the effect of the specific unsatisfied. Renier needled it directly into the two large brain-feeding arteries. The effect, for Rudisijl, was instant and devastating.

'The cloud was there for a reason,' the dying man moaned in his lower tone. 'We shouldn't have allowed this synthetic and needled clarity to drive it away. I was wrong! What can one do who has been as wrong as I was?'

Then he broke three octaves upward. He shrilled, he howled on the high key, he broke his terrified voice and choked down in heavy death râles. And he moaned words again in his lower tone:

'The animals haven't entered their post-everything age yet. They still have the capacity of belief. They believe we are gods. When the natural cloud in them was driven away and they looked for the first time clearly on the fact of death, they felt that they could propitiate us into giving them ultimate death-salvation. They prayed to us with stepped pyramids and bright objects and harping and singing. That's what all their promising activity was really about. But I am a post-person, and there is no one I can pray to. The normal death-calm is prevented in me by my own clarifying specific. Oh, it's the outright terror that cannot be tolerated either in sanity or in insanity.'

Those were the last understandable words that Rudisijl ever spoke. But, broken voice and all, he was pretty noisy during those last several minutes of his life. The clarifying specific had overcome the mind-cloud that ordinarily insulates against the fear of death, at the instant of death anyhow. Rudisijl had no insulation and no protection now. It was a stark and towering fear that followed him even into insanity.

Ghost-fears and night-horrors were parts of it, hysterical fear of falling was a part of it, strangulation was a part and being buried alive was a part, form-changes and walking corpses and intolerable loneliness were parts of it, and the temptation-choice between extinction and hell, and the choking fog that is a pursuing person.

And the other parts of it – No, no, no! There are aspects of the clarified and cloud-cleared death-vision that cannot –

It was a contorted animal terror that took over what had once been Rudisijl's face. It was a many-tongued para-animal, howling and rowling, that took over what had once been his voice. His eyes distended from the intolerable vision and became bursting-full nodules of blood. And they burst open literally with a gory gushing.

Rudisijl died in grey and deformed terror.

Christina

by

DAPHNE CASTELL

No wonder she dreams. Daphne Castell has been deputy librarian at the Imperial Forestry Institute; now she teaches ESN children, as well as evening classes on Effective Speaking and English for the Profoundly Deaf. She lives in Oxford, plays percussion in an orchestra, sings contralto in a choir, broadcasts on BBC, has 'three eccentric children and five evil cats', is interested in bell-ringing, traffic problems, drama, etc., and somehow found the time to study English under Tolkien.

Her work has appeared in Fantasy and Science Fiction, New Worlds, Amazing, Science Fantasy, *various anthologies (Elwood, Anne McCaffrey), and a host of journals. She dreams most of her plots (well, she needs some relaxation). She dreamed 'Christina', which made her weep: me too. But there is no lack of terror, as you'll see.*

It is sometimes difficult to believe, in times of war, and want, and miserable damage to children, in the existence of a just and loving God.

But it is quite impossible to believe that all this luxuriant growth of human life, each bud bursting out in continuous flow from the evolutionary tree, and each powered by a soul, is to go to waste, to be flushed away like so much useless sludge, down a huge drain-pipe. I have always refused to believe this; and I have refused to believe, too, that the vanishing beings who leave the world, withering in such quantities each day, do not leave behind them some indelible stain for other beings to discover, if they have power to discover.

Whether I am such a being, I do not know. I have lived in a house where I could not sleep for fear, and left it, to hear that next day it was burnt, and only one life saved. I have met a person whose hand I could not touch because it felt wet and sticky, as if it were streaming with something not to be seen; and later I have heard that he was to be tried for murder.

And I met Christina, whose very existence seemed to me for so long an injustice, that there have been times when I could not go to sleep for weeping about it.

When I went to live in the large stone house at the end of a small village in the Midlands, I did not think I was going to enjoy it much. I had been ill, and a close friend had died. I had lost some money, and I was out of touch, because of a disagreement with my family. But I had to live somewhere, and this was cheap, and in a healthy place. I would certainly grow stronger here, if not happier. I was writing, at the time, children's stories, which bored me, and I hoped that I might find some refreshment in a village atmosphere; some wind might blow through my dull, curtained mind telling me to enjoy once more what I was doing.

The house wasn't very agreeable in itself. It was a good size, the rooms were well-shaped, and the windows were wide and looked onto a large pleasant garden. But the rooms felt both cold and stuffy, and there was a general air of damp and depression about the place, as if it had not yet been left to go to seed, but might, one day soon.

I was merely renting it, however; and I could soon leave if I found that I couldn't settle in. I shared the house with another woman, a pleasant quiet countrywoman, a Mrs Crozier, middle-aged but with a smooth unlined face and strong hands. She had kept house for the family who had lived there earlier. She now had the upper storey of the house, and a small scullery-kitchen downstairs. She was a widow, used to the house, in spite of its changes; and apparently it had suited her to come to an arrangement with the owners and the agents, whereby she paid a small rent, and aired unused rooms and took care of the garden. There were only a few upper rooms, which were usually closed, and which neither I nor she had any use for. The garden was a large one – they allowed her to grow what she wanted there, and to sell what she didn't need in the neighbouring market-town. She grew a great variety of vegetables, and some flowers. It was a long walled garden, with small box edges round the beds, not very neat now that there was only one woman to look after them. The pigeons were a great trial to her, and she put up rows of fluttering cotton rags and tinkling silver bits of foil, on black thread, to keep them away. She managed very well, though – there were always vegetables to spare for me; and the borders of old-fashioned pinks flourished without the need for care and tending. On many mornings, I woke up to find the sun already hot on the borders below my window, and the spicy enchanting scent, gay and impertinent, yet with a hint of old-fashioned formality about it winding its way round my pillows.

Mrs Crozier had no desire to talk; and she never gossiped about the family that had gone. She would say 'Good morning' usually, but sometimes she would merely offer me an early lettuce, or a bunch of radishes, with a remote, rather absent-minded smile. She suited me very well as a neighbour.

I saw few other people, apart from the postman and the milkman. Bread we bought from the village shop, where it was freshly made, in large, smoke-blackened, ancient ovens every day except Sunday. On the Saturday, one bought two days' supply.

I don't think that village people actively avoided the house. It was rather as if they felt they should ignore it, that they didn't need to notice it, as part of their daily existence.

I can't remember a single person calling, even out of curiosity, for the first four months of my stay there.

I once asked Mrs Crozier why nobody came to visit her or to pay me a fact-finding call. I knew that she had friends, for I had often seen her chatting to them, in the shop, or on the corner of the street. She sometimes went out in the evenings, and I assumed that the whole of her social life was led in other people's houses, for she never entertained friends.

She hummed to herself in an embarrassed way for a moment or two, and then said that she supposed that people were too busy round here to spare time to go looking about for things. It was an odd phrase; but the ending of it was somehow the oddest part, for she hesitated over it, as if what she really meant to say was that people didn't go out of their way to look for trouble. Trouble of some sort, but of a very vague, unspecified nature, so vague that perhaps she wasn't even sure of its existence – or the people she spoke of weren't sure, perhaps.

I saw Christina first on a damp calm morning in late summer, when the sky was still sulky from an unexpected shower. She was standing in one of the garden beds, looking down at something, a thin, pale-haired, rather grubby little girl, of perhaps seven or eight. I opened the window, intending to call to her. I wasn't quite sure what – perhaps that she mustn't walk on the beds, perhaps that she would get muddy, and her mother would be angry.

She didn't hear the window open, apparently, though it stuck and creaked as I pushed at it; but she turned and walked away with unexpected abruptness, and disappeared round the corner of the house.

Oddly, the garden didn't look quite the same after she had gone. It was like one of those unconvincing photographs that have been touched up – you can tell where an outline has been removed, there is something missing, something inadequate.

I wondered, a little irritably, whether the children from the village were now going to adopt the habit of coming into the garden. It wasn't my garden, of course; if anyone had a claim to it, it was Mrs Crozier. But it was annoying to think of ball games, hasty feet, and persistent trebles beneath one's window.

I asked Mrs Crozier if she had seen the little girl playing in the garden, when I saw her in the afternoon. The damp had lifted, and the day had settled down into a fair, warm, rosy haze, a deliciously soft and fruitful time.

Mrs Crozier looked startled, I thought. Her smooth brow creased into two slanting lines.

'I didn't, no, miss.' She always insisted on calling me this. She had learnt that I had once taught in a school. To her way of thinking, it seemed, all teachers were 'miss'. It was an odd regression to childhood habits, and made me nostalgic sometimes for the crowded, recognisable life of the playground and the classroom. At least you knew where you were with them.

'A smallish, very fair-haired child, not very well looked after –' I persisted. 'About eight, perhaps, with rather a thin, thoughtful, obstinate face. She wore a pale green cotton dress.'

Mrs Crozier murmured something I couldn't hear under her breath, and her face went stiller and blanker than ever.

'No, miss. There wouldn't be any child playing in the garden that I know of. They don't generally come up by here.'

'Well, I saw her, so she must have taken a fancy to play here by herself,' I said, rather snappishly. 'I hope she's not going to make a habit of it.'

Mrs Crozier looked at me quietly, and her brows crinkled again. But all she said was, 'I hope not, either, miss.'

I sat down to my typewriter at the open window, and worked on, already a little ashamed of having let loose my temper about a child. Hadn't I always held in contempt those elderly ladies who write notes to their neighbours, complaining that the children are playing their nasty ball-games on the grass patch near the houses, may they be told to keep away, please?

As the day came softly on, the shadows stretched from the stunted apple trees and the luxuriant yews into my windows, and disturbed my mind with all sorts of odd patterns and imaginings. Afternoon drooped into evening, but I wasn't hungry, and didn't wish to stop work.

Scent came more strongly from the pinks, and my nostrils were pricked, too, by the heady smells of fresh earth, turned by Mrs Crozier in her digging, and the intoxication of crushed grass and clovers. The light continued to fade until tree trunks and box edges and leaves melted into the twilight glimmer which makes the whole out-of-doors into one big elusive patchwork.

I could hear some small repetitive noise after a while, but I was too much engrossed in what I was trying to do to identify it. Gradually, though, the idea crept into my mind that it was part of a human voice, just the upper edges of it, with the lower notes made inaudible by distance or muffling of some kind. Somebody, to judge by the repetition of the sound, and the monotony of it, was counting or reciting or going through some other demanding ritual.

It was one of those compulsive procedures which rouse one's curiosity to a pitch at which one feels almost inclined to join in.

I rose to look out of the darkened window. I could see very little, but I could hear more clearly; the tones sounded more desolate now, and I thought I could distinguish something like a sob from time to time:

'Oh kitten – Oh kitten!' I could hear, and then: 'Oh Mummy! Oh Mummy!' A child, I thought, lost, or run away – having been punished perhaps. By straining my eyes, I thought I could just make out a figure at the very end of the garden. Someone was evidently pacing up and down there, turning and making measured paces, then hopping solemnly, it seemed, for I could just see the unsteady gait, and the point of a raised knee. 'Oh kitten – Oh kitten!' Then a stride and a hop and a turn. Then 'Oh Mummy – Oh Mummy!' and another pace, and a hop, and a turn. Then more chanting: 'He's gone now, he's gone now, it's all done, he's gone now.' I know as much as any human being about the compulsive acts we are forced to perform by the clock inside us. But there was something about this extraordinary ritual that I had to stop, for the sheer sorrow in it, the feeling that I was unable to bear it any longer myself.

So I rose and ran outside; but when I stood clear of the door, I could see that the performance had stopped, and the performer had gone.

I had very little doubt that it was the little girl I had seen in the morning; and I thought it probable that Mrs Crozier knew her. There was evidently some sort of family trouble, perhaps a village scandal; and Mrs Crozier would keep quiet about it, and probably do all she could to extend to the child an unobtrusive helping hand. She wouldn't gossip; as I knew, she wasn't that sort of woman. And if there was any trouble in the village, I would hardly like to get involved in it myself. Yet the child hadn't looked actually ill-treated, though she had a certain air of forlorn independence that children do acquire when they are not used to any form of concentrated attention from adults. I am actively unhappy when I have any suspicion that children may be suffering; adults can usually look after their own well-being very much better than people suspect. But children are always victims of adult dictation and deception. They are constantly being forced to accept terms for which they have no reference or means of judgement. So I had to find out from Mrs Crozier whether this little girl was being ill-treated; or, something rather different, whether she was not being treated quite well enough.

It was a major task, as I could have foreseen. Mrs Crozier first took on the appearance of believing that I must have made a mistake – that there could have been no child there, either the first time or the second. When I said firmly that in that case I must be going mad, and that I would call on the local doctor to tell him the full story, and to arrange for tests of my eyesight, hearing, and psychological state, she looked very much alarmed. I didn't know whether she was worried at the thought that I might be persuaded into doubting my sanity; or whether she was worried at what I might actually tell the doctor.

She said that she hadn't actually seen anyone herself, and that she didn't recognise the description – and this, I could tell at once, was a lie. She knew the child, and she wasn't used to lying. But, she said, feebly enough, I might have seen the grandchild of old Mrs Baines, who was lying very sick down the road. Her daughter had come, with her own children, from London, to nurse her until her death, which was reputed to be not far off.

I believed this, for it seemed possible that there was something wrong with one of the London children, and that Mrs Crozier didn't want to talk about it; I believed it, until I walked down into the village one morning, and saw the whole of Mrs Baines' London family gathered outside the post-office, talking excitedly about how bad she had been taken during the night, and how they were just off to get the doctor now. There were five children – two tall thin sons, and three daughters, all small, rosy, black-browed, and two of them on the verge of young womanhood. I have never been able to imagine how they all struggled into old Mrs Baines' small cottage.

But none of them, by any stretch of imagination, could have been the thin eight-year-old I had seen in the garden.

I was all the more exasperated, because I couldn't quite get the child out of my mind after the mournful recital I had heard.

It was as if I had to carry the burden of constantly worrying about her, as if I had some kind of a duty to perform to her, or for her. Mrs Crozier was no help at all. When I told her that I had seen the Baines' family, and that they were not in the least like our garden visitor, she retired into herself like a hermit-crab. She would only reiterate that she was sure she couldn't help me. She didn't know, she couldn't help me.

A feverish day of bending over my typewriter, and trying urgently to coax some sort of sense and pleasure out of its sharp black letters didn't help. On a scurrying evening of chilly wind, whipping unexpectedly round corners of the house and drawing ragged edges of cloud across the slice of a new moon, I went to bed early, hot ,worried, and restless. The wind rose to a full storm before midnight, and brought with it occasional vast, silent, window-wide flickers of lightning, and a rattle of quiet thunder below the horizon. Some unfortunate people were having a genuine Turneresque masterpiece of a thunderstorm. Not us, fortunately, but I still couldn't sleep properly, though I dozed, and turned over, and dozed again. The atmosphere was stretched taut and dangerous as an electric fence. I began to think that a thunderstorm would be almost a relief – if something didn't happen, the whole fabric of creation was going to rip.

There was no real darkness in the room, no sense of shadow or anything lurking, and most of the furniture was clear to my sight; so that I cannot say at all how it was that one moment she was not there, and the next I saw her. The sight of a small hand stretched out in a friendly comforting gesture was as unexpected as a scream on a sunlit lawn.

'I don't like thunder,' she said, the child from the garden. She shivered, and I could see her thin shoulder-bones. 'Do you?'

I didn't know how to answer, and if I had been able to, my dry tongue, sticking to my palate, would have made it inaudible.

Communication seems such an easy thing; but most of us know already what we are talking to. There is no precedent for speaking in what was, until she came, an empty room.

She came forward, and I still couldn't say anything. Her pale, rather grubby face frowned, and she said, 'Why are you there? Why don't you move? Aren't you uncomfortable? The bed's over there. The kitten used to lie on it, sometimes.' Then her face shadowed, and she whispered something inaudible and looked as if she were going to cry. She began moving backwards, and my tongue was loosened, and I cried out: 'It's all right – it's all right, don't go away! No, I don't like thunder, either.'

She seemed to hesitate. Then she whispered: 'The bed's over there. Why don't you –?' The window brightened with sheet lightning, and dulled again, and she flickered out like a blown match.

I sat with my bedclothes clutched round me, staring at the space which she had occupied. I didn't know how to think or move for a few moments. I could feel my tongue moving slowly round my lips, and then I found myself rubbing my feet softly, for they were cold, and saying again to myself: 'It's all right, it's all right.'

The most extraordinary thing was that after this, I dropped immediately into a deep exhausted sleep, and woke to a bright, wet morning, streaming with heavy dew and sun, with a feeling of relief. I now knew what it was I had been looking for, and I knew what was wrong, and why, though I didn't yet know what to do about it. But I had a deep conviction that that would be shown to me.

I refused to use, even in my thoughts, the silly word 'ghost'. It is simply a name allotted – it means so little. This creature, whoever she was, was not a living being, in the sense that things occurred to her, or occurred where she was, that couldn't have happened with a living being. That was the only difference, and I was conscious enough of it, as I sat over my breakfast, to be sure that I would see the child again, that she was not a shuddering phenomenon – and most of all, that I must see Mrs Crozier.

I found her trenching up round the bared roots of some shrubs. She pushed her hair back from her brows, and looked round at me, but didn't uncurl her back. She seemed to know what I wanted from her, and she was unwilling to give it. Her face looked strained and exhausted and troubled, middle-aged for the first time since I had begun to know her.

'Well, miss?' she said, warily.

'Mrs Crozier, you must tell me. The little girl – did you

know her? Was she a child of yours? Of a friend of yours?'

'Oh, the child!' she cried, flinging out her arms in a despairing gesture. 'Are you on at that again, miss? Begging your pardon, and not wishing to be rude, but can't you leave it as it is?' And then she whispered: 'What made you say "was"? Did you know, then?'

'Since last night.' I nodded. 'She was in my room – and then she wasn't. There was lightning – you must have seen it – and she flashed out of sight, exactly like the moment when the dark comes back again. Who was she, Mrs Crozier?'

She whimpered at me, and wouldn't say anything for a moment. It was an astonishing descent into abjection, for one who had her own kind of complete dignity; but I could feel that it wasn't fear of what silly people call the supernatural – as if there were only one kind of nature. No, she rubbed her perplexed head, and dug frantic heels into the ground, as if driven by some desperate indecision that terrified her because she was so unused to not being able to make up her own mind.

I tried to help, but I didn't know whether I might not perhaps make things worse.

'Someone you knew well? You were very fond of her, and her family?'

Scorn flashed at me from her dark eyes for a withering second, and then she dropped her head again, and nibbled nervously at a finger-tip. Something came into my mind.

'What happened about the kitten? Is it something to do with a kitten? Is that what's – what's making her – what's troubling her?' I didn't know the right words. 'Is it what's keeping her here?'

This time real fear peered up at me. She whispered: 'Did she say –? You heard, then, you really heard?'

'And I saw her,' I insisted. 'Do you mean you haven't seen her?'

She looked darkly at the shrubs. 'Sometimes – sometimes I've been sure I heard her – only I said to myself no good was to come of that, and all I'd be doing was troubling them. They were very good to me, about this place, you see, miss, and her parents are dead, too.'

'Then she died here? And she's come back – looking for the kitten?'

She shook her head vehemently, and gave a half-vexed cry, almost of surrender, as if it was to be a relief to tell me what I wanted to know. 'I don't know what it could be, miss. If it was her mother, now –' she stopped, and her face darkened again, and an uneasy little ripple ran over her whole body. It was evident that she had disliked or feared the child's mother. 'No, she didn't die here. But her mother did. They were an uneasy, misfitted, upside-down family. Her dad thought the whole world of Christina.'

That was the first time I had heard her name.

'Her mother wasn't all there, I think. People said she'd liked a drink too much, and been cured of it, and her brain had never been quite the same. I never saw anything of that about her, but she was odd, no denying it. And she was very dependent on those two, the little girl and the father. Seemed as if she needed them a lot more than they did her. You couldn't help but feel sorry for her. They went their own ways, because he was a busy man, and a learned one, and though he was fond of the little girl, like I told you, he didn't spend much time with her. But you could tell how fond he was when they were together, and you could see Christina was fond of him back; only she hadn't any time for her mother. Not that you could blame her, except that it seemed unnatural. But she was a spiteful, sly woman, her mother.'

I could picture it quite clearly, the whole miserable parody of family life. Much better never to have had a child, than to have alienated it, and known that – poor wretched woman, with her oddness, her malice, her slyness that had made Mrs Crozier fear and dislike her.

'What about the kitten?' I asked her. She didn't seem to hear me at first, for when she answered, her reply bore no relationship to what I had asked her.

'She killed herself, the mother. She hung herself in that big cupboard in the room at that end of the house, the old stone larder. There was a big iron hook in the back of the door. Christina found her.'

The idea sickened me – I turned faint with distress for the child, coming upon that sagging shapeless bundle, dark, swollen, inhuman, as the face must have been. Mrs Crozier was going on.

'And she hardly said a word, the child. Came to me – I was working here, you know – and found me in the big kitchen, where I was kneading away at a pan of dough. She stood on the doorsill, and said: "Mrs Crozier, Mummy's hanging up there, and I can't get her off. She looks awful, Mrs Crozier." And then she dropped down in a heap, and I was nearly off my head, not knowing what to do, whether to pick her up, or to run and see what the woman had done now. But I couldn't leave the child, how could I? I had to wait with her, until someone came – they were expecting a coal delivery, but a boy from the village came up before then, or I don't know what I'd have done. He was away, and I couldn't get Christina to come round or wake up properly. I thought she was dying, too – oh, I don't know what I thought, alone there in the kitchen, with her all flopped out, white as death and only just breathing. Then the boy came, and I left him with her, and went to see. It was an awful thing, miss. And I couldn't get her down, for she was a big heavy woman – only I left white streaks from the dough, all over her clothes, from trying to lift her enough to loosen the rope. She was almost touching the floor. It was a big door, but not that big. She'd jumped off a stool.'

'That – that can't have been an easy way out.'

'No. I reckon she'd strangled to death, not broke her neck. I haven't ever forgotten her face, from that day to this. They always say that people that kill themselves regret it, the moment that they're dying. I could swear to it she did, poor thing – poor thing!'

'In a way, Mrs Crozier, I find it difficult to be sorry for her. I was thinking of the child. Of course, her mother must have been unbalanced. But – not to have thought of the child, or her father – what they would find –'

'There was ill-feeling enough in her, miss, for her to have thought of that, and still gone on and done it. I still say, poor thing, for there was so much misery in that family, with them wandering apart from her like that, you have to feel sorry for her. The kitten – well, miss, I think the child could tell herself why her mother had done that. No one ever rightly gets into a child's mind. But she loved the kitten. And she knew her mother was jealous of it. I always believed Christina felt somehow she owed her mother a make-weight for what she'd had to do. She'd had to do it, says Christina to herself, may be – I'm just guessing, miss – because no one could manage to love her. Christina loved the kitten. So one day, she took it down to the pond, and tied a brick round its neck, and put it, very gently, in the water. Then she ran away crying fit to die, the tears blinding down her face. She never saw me coming round the end of the wall, and I didn't dare call out to her. But I saw it all – that's how I know how tenderly she put it in the water. She wouldn't know how else to kill the little thing. My breath was nearly choking me, but I went down by that pond on my knees, and stuck my arm in, and got myself all over green slime and mud, and I got the kitten out alive. Only then, miss, how could I give it back to Christina? I was fair stuck – I had something of an idea of what was in her mind, but I couldn't tell for sure. So I gave it to a friend of mine, a quiet woman who lives down the other end of the village. She's a widow, too, and doesn't talk to folk much.'

'So the kitten's alive? And she never saw it again? She thought it was dead.'

'That's right. And that afternoon was her mother's funeral. And it wasn't long after that they went away.'

'They went away? But then she's not dead?'

'Oh, yes, she's dead, miss. Not that I ever saw her myself,

again, after that. But she died, they told me, in the 'plane crash, with her father; he'd thought a holiday would be a good thing, for both of them. She'd dwindled away, after her mother's death, and he thought it was that. Well, it could have been. She used to wake shrieking. But I always thought myself it was the kitten. She might have thought herself that she was to blame for her mother's death – such a baby as she was. But it was the kitten she killed with her own two hands, or thought she had. Have you ever killed a thing, miss?' I'd run over a duckling once, on a farm path; I knew what she meant. 'I'd have given it back to her, if only I could. But how could I, miss? It was a – it was some sort of sacrifice she'd been looking for. If she knew the kitten was all right, what was she going to do next?'

It was a strange, crazy question, in a dream-like atmosphere. The sky seemed to close round us and hold us apart from the world, suffocatingly dark, although it was a bright, still morning. I shook my head to clear it.

'I don't know, Mrs Crozier. But what is it now? Is it the kitten she's looking for? Or her mother? Or is she just held here somehow?' Mrs Crozier shook her head.

'She was asleep, under drugs, when her father took her away from here. The 'plane crashed on take-off, only a few hours after. She might have been still asleep. It can't be her mother, miss, they weren't close, and surely the dead don't feel guilty? Not her – not Christina?'

I said stumblingly, 'Did you ever wonder whether she doesn't – she doesn't know where she is, what she's doing? Whether she doesn't even know she's dead? She sees things as they were, I think. She could see the bed as it used to be, in a different place.' I couldn't say any more, and neither could Mrs Crozier. We stared at each other with heavy eyes, as laden and exhausted as if we'd been climbing some steep path; and then, mutually separating we went our ways, and kept as far apart as we could, for the rest of that day.

I didn't know what to do with myself. I didn't want food. I

felt enormously guilty, as though I had stolen someone's secrets. I couldn't settle to write, and I wandered in and out of the house.

At dusk, after I had eaten a piece of cheese and an apple, I sat down on a bench outside my window, and tried to interest myself in a pocket chess-set. I have never been good at the game, but I've always loved it for its infinite possibilities, its wide wanderings of variety, and the individuality of its pieces. As I put my hand on the black knight to move him, and fork a queen and rook, I saw out of the corner of my eye the same sort of movement that you see when a tiny fly is caught in a loose strand of hair, or when something is dangling too close to you to be focused – something not seen, but noticed.

Then the small thin voice whispered, right at my shoulder, 'It's better now, the thunder's gone, hasn't it?' And at once I wasn't frightened, but filled with an immense anxiety to do the right thing.

I kept my head bent and said in the same soft monotone, 'Yes, it's warm and comfortable, and the sun's only just gone.'

'Who are you? I'm Christina. You're in my house, aren't you? My house is funny now. Things move about, very quickly. Have you been here a long time?'

If someone, years ago, when I first knew that I could taste the unusual, had suggested seriously to me that ghosts might have asked questions, I might have been incredulous and angry. But what else could this being do? At least she could see and hear me, and I might help her, if she needed help. If any God existed, why wasn't he making a way for this lost child? – or was I to be the way?

'Not long,' I said. 'I like your house, Christina. My name is Ann.'

'Have you seen my kitten?' So it was the kitten. 'He should be here. I know he should be here. Some things aren't, but he should be. I hope they don't cut these bushes. Daddy says they will, but I hope not. I like them. There are nests, and I can crawl through underneath.'

It was strange to watch, while she bent and seemed to slide through something that wasn't there, pushing things back, and easing herself past. There were no bushes at that corner.

'Christina,' I said, 'Mrs Crozier loves you, doesn't she?' I had nearly said 'loved'. How in Heaven's name does one tell a child she is dead?

The shadowed face glowed, and became clearer. 'Yes, she's good and nice. When I grow up, I'm going to –' she looked dimly troubled, and stopped. Then she came close to me, really near. 'Mummy's dead, and the kitten's dead, too. Why isn't it here?' Then she flickered out of existence, out of sight again.

After that, within the next few weeks, I saw her often, and Mrs Crozier saw her too, I am convinced, though she wouldn't talk to me again about it. Christina was sometimes silent, sometimes talking, sometimes singing to herself the strange little chant, with movements that I had heard first. It was as if she had gained a sudden confidence – can a ghost have confidence?

One thing that troubled me badly was the growing unpleasantness at the end of the house where Mrs Crozier said the mother had killed herself. I could only suppose that as I had grown more sensitive to Christina's presence, so the other things that might remain with the house made themselves clearer to me. Once I had to go into the old stone larder in broad clear day, to get the milk that was kept cool there, and the end of the room nearest the cupboard seemed to me to throb steadily away, pulsing with near-darkness, like a kind of wicked power-house. You could almost scent the wrong in it. It might be auto-suggestion – I kept telling myself that I knew too much of the story, that I would obviously think round it. But I knew that the end of the room was black and sticky with some kind of ambush, and that the child should never go near it. As it happened, I never saw her at that end of the house at all. She was more often in the garden than anywhere else. I told Mrs Crozier about the throbbing in the old larder, and though she said nothing, she stopped putting the milk in there to cool.

This began a very unhappy time for me. I felt wretchedly helpless, and burdened with the feeling that it all rested upon me. I was afraid of the thing, whatever it was, in the larder, though I certainly did not believe that all suicides would be automatically damned, and therefore out to destroy vengefully. And there were times when I could not bear to think of Christina's existence at all, or the fact that she should be here, not knowing why, and not able to receive help from those who most wanted, and were least able, to give it.

I wept often, in bed at night; no child should still be lonely after death — it wasn't right or just. But the worst pressure of all was the growing feeling that the only thing I could do for her was to kill the kitten. I was perhaps a little crazy by now with the strangeness of it all, and Mrs Crozier was no help. But Christina had tried to kill the kitten, and it wasn't dead; and at least if I killed it, whether it released her or not, she might have company. The only company of her sort now was whatever might be brooding in the old stone larder, and I would rather not think of that. I knew the kitten quite well by this time — I had often gone down to see it, with Mrs Crozier's friend at the other side of the village. It was a pretty, half-grown wild little thing now, a nondescript colour, with a small head and a long tail.

It seemed reasonable that I should take the responsibility of killing the creature, since Christina hadn't shrunk from attempting it.

I watched it for most of one dull, hot afternoon, when things seemed to be rotting rather than ripening; but I slunk home at last, unable to make up my mind how to do it.

I dragged my feet up the drive, feeling that I must go and talk to Mrs Crozier, that I must get something out of her, some kind of assistance. She couldn't refuse if I put it to her that we must help Christina, I reasoned.

I came round the corner of the house into the main garden, looking for her, but she wasn't there. I knew she was in, for the vicar's wife had called earlier to see if she would give a hand with some village jaunt or other, and she had refused. She had too much to do about the house and garden, she had said, and she must get it done before the weather broke. She wasn't in the herb garden, or round the back in the yard, or with the poultry. I called up her stairs, and into the window of the kitchen. I couldn't hear her or any sound at all. Christina had not been visible for some days, and the house was as soundless as a museum.

I shall never know what made me peer through the little grimy window of the old larder, but I did, lifting myself high on my toes to do so. At first it was shadowed, then things grew clearer. The cupboard door, just inside and on the opposite wall from the window, was open, and Mrs Crozier lay on her back near it.

The whole room was absolutely empty, clear, unmarked – swept and garnished. Without thinking, I ran round to the side door, clattered over the broad grey flags of the short passage, and opened the door to the old larder. I went inside and stopped, almost suffocated. There was nothing to see, but something was drawing the breath from me as I stood. I had to lean, literally, against this huge menacing suction, fight for every breath, staggering towards Mrs Crozier. The air brightened round me till it sparkled, and rims of light formed round my eyes, as the blood was cramped into the innermost corners of my head. Mrs Crozier looked tiny, small, and drained. I thought she was withering, minute by minute, under the unbearable pressure. Inch by inch I struggled to her, feeling myself diminish as I went. It was like trying to enter bodily the wrong end of a half-rolled coil of carpet. The coil narrowed down towards the deadly cupboard, and I tried to drag Mrs Crozier back away from it. She might have been made of bronze, anchored and riveted to the floor. I felt myself slipping and sagging beside her, when there was a sudden lightening of pressure, and the outer door swung open. Christina came in. She had something in her arms. Whatever was holding us withdrew for a tentative moment, and Mrs Crozier groaned and moved.

'It's all right, Mrs Crozier, I've got the kitten,' cried the child's thin voice joyfully. Attention temporarily taken from us, whatever was holding us moved and slid sideways, towards Christina, leaving us unpinned, but too stunned to rise.

'Don't!' called Christina, sharply, yet almost negligently. She bent her head down to her arms, and then raised it; and I heard a man's voice call somewhere beyond the house. It sounded weary, but casually authoritative.

'Come on now, Christina. Come on.'

'All right, Daddy, coming. Come on, kitten.' And she began to walk away, and away, somehow moving the walls with her own movement, so that we could see her still moving for an incalculable distance. Then there was something like a great silent clap, the soundless implosion of emptiness, and we were alone in the kitchen, getting up and gasping, white and exhausted, but perfectly well and sound in mind.

There was no sound, no sense of any pressure. The room was sweet and clean and unpossessed.

It wasn't until next morning that one of the boys from the village brought the news that Christina's little half-grown cat, sunning itself on its new owner's piece of grass, had been run over by a car, going astray from the road. It had died at once.

The Case of James Elmo Freebish

by

JOSEPH F. PUMILIA

Joseph F. Pumilia (1945–) lives in Austin, Texas. He has been a reporter, but is now a freelance writer who also does work as copywriter and artist for an advertising agency. His science fiction and horror stories have been variously anthologised.

With Bill Wallace he founded the Esoteric Order of Dagon, a Lovecraft-oriented amateur press association, and writes articles about (and stories by) Mortimer Morbius Moamrath, 'eccentric New England writer of bizarre and inept horror fiction'. Pumilia's deadpan humour and love of horror are well represented in the following. The old EC horror comics (Tales From The Crypt and so on) will never look quite the same again.

Now you just know something bad's going to happen to James Elmo Freebish, because he's just sitting there in his favourite chair, note pad in his lap, with a silly look on his face as he thinks about the funny look on little Janie Ferguson's face as her daddy's head went *bumpity, bumpity, bumpity* down the thirteen steps of her front porch. There's *no way* this story can end without something *horrible* happening to James Elmo, you say. And you're *right*!

Because not only is James Elmo a murderer, but he has no *feelings*. He doesn't care about poor orphaned Janie. And to make it worse, he thinks it's *funny*! He even wrote a limerick about it:

> *Why'd I hack off his head with a sword?*
> *I can put it into one word.*
>   *Because, you see,*
>   *'Twas due to ennui.*
> *But now, I'm no longer bored.*

Limericks – that was James Elmo's passion. With some people it's crossword puzzles, or mah-jong, or string sculpture, but James Elmo's sole leisure time activity was composing limericks. Mrs Freebish, or Claire, as we'll call her, looked down on James Elmo for this reason. She had better things to do in her spare time, like counting blackmail money. Whenever her husband was sitting in his easy chair with his note pad, composing limericks, she would sneer and say: 'Simple pleasures for simple minds.'

That always got a rise out of him. Simple pleasures for simple minds. How he hated that sentence! How many times had he heard it? Six thousand? Ten thousand? Whenever he heard it, he would recite to himself a limerick he had composed:

> *The disposal of Claira's remains*
> *Was a puzzle exceedingly strange.*
>   *Not even the flue*
>   *Was o'erlooked for a clew,*
> *But all they could find were her brains.*

Lately he had been so aggravated by her remarks that he had been turning his talents to other deadly verses, such as:

> *The maid's piercing scream split the air*
> *When she found what was left of Miss Claire.*
>   *There were gobbets of ooze*
>   *In her clothes, in her shooze,*
> *And puddles all over the stair.*

Tonight he had turned out another one, a bit more imaginative:

> *There was a maiden named Claire*
> *Who lived at the top of the stair.*
> *She bought her a squid*
> *For only five quid,*
> *And it strangled her then and there.*

And if the truth be known, it was not only in fanciful poems that he pictured her dead. He had begun to think about ways of accomplishing it in reality.

So James Elmo sits there in the chair, thinking about how to murder his wife, even as she rummages around in the kitchen making domestic wifely noises. What he doesn't know is that she is looking for the biggest, sharpest butcher knife she has, because she has plans of her own for James Elmo. And here she comes, walking up behind him on tiptoe, and – oops! She trips on the edge of the rug. But these things all work out for the best, because she falls with both hands holding the knife and doesn't chicken out like she probably would have. James Elmo had always told her she was a fraidy cat. And had James Elmo ever chickened out? No, he hadn't, not even when Mr Ferguson said he was going to the police because he didn't have any more money to pay blackmail, and besides, he'd paid his debt to society years ago, and if anyone wanted to spread the word he was an ex-convict, well let them, and anyhow little Janie needed that operation or she'd die of what her mother died of.

But James Elmo was adamant, and he didn't chicken out, not even when old man Ferguson pulled the gun on him and tried to make a citizen's arrest. James Elmo just jumped sideways and grabbed that old Japanese samurai sword Mr Ferguson had brought back from the war.

And he didn't chicken out. No sir! He just lopped off Ferguson's head with one chop, and it rolled across the floor and out the front door and down the steps, *bumpity*, *bumpity*, *bumpity* thirteen times. Those Japs sure knew how to make swords!

Well, likewise Claire wasn't about to chicken out now, not with her 190 pounds falling thirty-two feet per second *per second* right onto James Elmo. But the worst part was that split second before she connected, when James Elmo turned around and saw her coming at him. And he just had time to open his mouth into a startled O as the blade THUNKed into his heart, going straight through it and into his spine.

Well, he'll never write another limerick, Claire tells herself. And James Elmo looks back at her in outraged surprise and he looks so funny Claire has to laugh. But James Elmo won't talk, no more than little Janie who'd been struck dumb by the sight of her daddy's head rolling down the steps like a rubber ball.

Now Claire has to make her husband's death look like an accident, and this is the easy part. She just sits him back in his chair and places around and about him his gun-cleaning supplies – oil, cotton wads, and so on. And she stands his favourite shotgun between his legs as if he's cleaning it, and she puts a shell in the gun, and she puts his hand on the trigger. And she pulls the trigger, eyes averted.

And now nobody'll ever find the hole in James Elmo's chest made by the butcher knife. Because James Elmo doesn't *have* a chest any more.

We'll pass over the tragic scenes that follow: the funeral, the weeping relatives and friends, the tender sight of little Janie presenting a single petunia plucked from an adjacent grave at James Elmo's coffin.

So Claire went home to bed and took a sleeping pill and a dry martini, and she read herself to sleep with a travel folder on Europe, secure in the belief she'd seen the last of James Elmo and his limericks.

But of course, she has not seen the last of him. We wouldn't let him off that easily, would we?

But before the corpse of a murdered man can return to take revenge on its killer, there is one condition that must be fulfilled. It must *not* be *embalmed*.

That's the reason so few corpses take revenge these days. Embalmed corpses just don't cut it as far as revenge is concerned. They may have the will, but all that formaldehyde sure puts a damper on things.

Fortunately – or unfortunately, depending on who you're rooting for – kindly old Mr Moamrath, the undertaker, decided that James Elmo was just too far gone for that sort of thing. There was just no point in it. It was going to be a closed casket ceremony, and even if he did pump the body full of embalming fluid, it would just gush out the hole in its chest. And do you know how much embalming fluid costs?

It costs a lot. Especially if you're poor, like Mr Moamrath.

So Mr Moamrath didn't embalm James Elmo Freebish. He just stuffed a little cotton and sawdust into the hole in his chest and sewed him up. Then he sealed the casket with an airtight seal and made sure it was doubly locked.

Why doubly locked? Because, you see, when you seal an unembalmed body in an airtight casket, there's something you have to be on guard against. The pressure of the gases of decomposition tends to build up, and sometimes the coffin *explodes*. Mr Moamrath, an ardent student of the history of undertaking, was well aware of this fact. For, centuries ago when the first Queen Elizabeth was laid unembalmed inside a lead crypt, that very thing happened to *her*. The lid just blew right off, and the poor queen was never so shaken up in her *life*, so it was *fortunate* she was dead or she'd have died of embarrassment!

But Mr Moamrath knew the funeral was going to be a quick one, and there would really be no chance for James Elmo to decay to any great extent before he was buried under six feet of heavy dirt. But he didn't reckon on an inebriated gravedigger, who decided what the hell, who's to know? And buried James Elmo under *two feet* of not-so-solid earth.

One night, about a week after the corpse had been planted, there was a sort of explosion in the cemetery.

It was just a sort of WHOOMP! and not an ear-splitting blast. Well, the next thing James Elmo Freebish knows is that he is up in a tree, looking down into a black hole.

How did I get here? he wonders. Then he remembers the last thing he'd seen – Claire lunging at him with the butcher knife. That would have made his blood boil – if he had any. So the first thing he does is climb down and brush off his suit. When he does this, the suit nearly comes off right there, because it's all open in the back.

It's not a real suit at all, he tells himself. It's more like those false suits old Moamrath puts on the –

And now he notices the tombstone.

Why, I must be dead! he concludes correctly.

Naturally his heart – figuratively speaking – begins to swell with thoughts of revenge. She can't do this to me, he thinks to himself. I'll make her sorry. Immediately a limerick occurs to him, the finest of his career:

> *The corpse returned from the grave*
> *To get the revenge he craved.*
> *The murd'rer he slew*
> *And flushed down the loo,*
> *Although that was simply depraved.*

Turning towards his home, James Elmo took a step forward. And fell on his face.

See, his right foot just dropped off.

Well, he *was* a rotting corpse, after all.

It took him quite a while to tie his foot back on with his shoe-laces. And by the time he'd reached Orlando Street, his other foot began showing signs of looseness at the ankle. And the mortification of his spinal tendons gave him a sort of forward hunch. His clothes weren't in good shape either, being torn and dusty from the explosion. And the colony of maggots in his left leg – well, it was a good thing his nerves were rotted away or the pain would be terrible.

Then he ran into a low tree limb and found that it hurt. *Those* nerves weren't rotted!

But the hacking cough is the worst, he thinks. The irritating tickle stays with him as he plods onward. It feels as though my lungs are full of sawdust and cotton, he says.

A further annoyance is that they did not bury him with his eyeglasses. Did they suppose his astigmatism would regress spontaneously merely because he was dead? A direct result of this is that his first choice of houses is wrong.

You can imagine elderly Mrs Gains sitting there with her tabby cat, Alfred, enjoying a wee bit of medicinal brandy. And the door flies open and in comes poor James Elmo. And when he opens his mouth to apologise, *his tongue falls out*.

Let's hope Mr Moamrath doesn't neglect to embalm poor old Mrs Gains.

It's the wee hours of the morning as James Elmo finally finds the right house. Without his glasses it's hard to be sure, but he is finally satisfied, because he ripped his rotting flesh on the thorns of Claire's prize rose-bushes. He tries to open the door. It's locked. He remembers the ladder behind the garage, and his putrefying lips curve in a wicked smile. He walks around the house, pausing only to retrieve a loose rib that drops from his shirt, and beat off the scowling dog who runs out to claim it.

It is difficult to position the ladder beneath his wife's window with both his wrists and elbow joints threatening to go out, but even in death the tendons are tough, and at last it is done. Now comes the arduous task of ascending the rungs. James Elmo applies himself diligently, but halfway up – bad luck! His right foot gives away again and falls into the flower bed. At least it fell into her prize roses, he tells himself.

The taste of this small Pyrrhic victory spurs him on, and before half an hour passes, he has made his way to the top. Thank goodness I don't have any breath to be out of, he sighs.

But it was the nagging cough that did him in. Just as he was going to work on the screen latch with a rusty screwdriver, the cough hit him. Down he went, fifteen feet in all, to smash into the driveway below.

There was a sickening snap as his head flew off and rolled across the driveway into a hedge against the Ferguson house. James Elmo was horribly aware of all this, of course, and when his head rolled to a stop, he could, by straining his eyes, see his broken body lying at the base of the ladder.

The dog was back now. James Elmo watched helplessly as it pulled a tibia loose and ran away with it. As he lay there through the night, the dog came back again and again, bringing along some of its friends, and by dawn the body was almost completely disposed of, except for a few scraps of cloth and a metatarsal or two.

And the head, of course.

James Elmo's head lay there unnoticed for a long time. He was still horribly conscious. He wondered how long it would take before he completely dissolved into dust. He wondered if the hot summer air had preserved him like a mummy.

How many days was it before he was found? Thirteen? Two weeks anyhow. The dogs must have buried his body all over town by now, those parts they haven't eaten.

It is late afternoon as Mrs Gains' orphaned tabby comes into the bushes where James Elmo lies. The cat sniffs at him, then disdainfully kicks him away as it prepares to . . . well, we needn't go into that.

James Elmo rolls onto the lawn, near the edge of the driveway.

An hour later a shadow falls across his myopic gaze. Two hands reach down and lift him up and he discovers himself to be looking into the blank, dull-eyed face of little Janie Ferguson. What was she doing back here at her old homestead? Homesick, probably.

It was the way she *smiled* at him that gave him the creeps.

He tried to cry out, but it was no use. There was no voice-box, and besides, his jaw muscles had turned to the consistency of old rubber tyres.

Where is she taking me? he wonders. Now he feels the vibrations as she climbs up stairs. He counts the jolts. One, two, three . . . eleven, twelve, thirteen. Now what? Oh, no!

Bumpity, bumpity, bumpity . . . Thirteen times.

Down the stairs he bounced, just like a rubber ball. And it hurt. *Those* nerves hadn't rotted away!

Then, up the steps again.

Yes, it didn't take much to amuse little Janie.

Bumpity, bumpity, bumpity . . .

Not the way she was now.

Bumpity, bumpity, bumpity . . .

Simple pleasures for simple minds.

The Hunting Ground

by

DAVID DRAKE

David Drake (1945–) almost gave up writing horror because of the recent lack of markets: which would have been a pity. He achieved a BA in History and Latin at the University of Iowa; was attached as an interrogator to the 11th Armored Cavalry Regiment in Vietnam, and is now Assistant Town Attorney for Chapel Hill, North Carolina.

In 1966 he sent August Derleth 'what I believed to be a story and he rather kindly referred to as a fair outline'. Under Derleth's guidance he sold Arkham House several tales, before Derleth's death closed that market temporarily. He began to write science fiction – reluctantly, but successfully: his work has appeared in Analog, Fantasy and Science Fiction, *and* Galaxy (*his anti-war* Hammer's Slammers *series*). *But even more than fantasy, his first love is horror: and this is his best and most frightening story to date.*

The patrol car's tyres hissed on the warm asphalt as it pulled to the kerb beside Lorne. 'What you up to, snake?' asked the square-bodied policeman. The car's rumbling idle and the whirr of its air-conditioner through the open window filled the evening.

Lorne smiled and nodded the lighted tip of his cigarette. 'Sitting on a stump in my yard, watching cops park on the wrong side of the street. What're you up to, Ben?'

Instead of answering, the policeman looked hard at his

friend. They were both in their late twenties; the man in the car stocky and dark with a close-cropped moustache; Lorne slender, his hair sand-coloured and falling across his neck brace.

'Hurting, snake?' Ben asked softly.

'Shit, four years is enough to get used to anything,' the thinner man said. Though Lorne's eyes were on the chime tower of the abandoned Baptist church a block down Rankin Street, his mind was lost in the far past. 'You know, some nights I sit out here for a while instead of going to bed.'

Three cars in quick succession threw waves of light and sound against the rows of ageing houses. One blinked its high beams at the patrol car briefly, blindingly. 'Bastard,' Ben grumbled without real anger. 'Well, back to the war against crime.' His smile quirked. 'Better than the last war they had us fighting, hey?'

Lorne finished his cigarette with a long drag. 'Hell, I don't know, sarge. How many jobs give you a full pension after two years?'

'See you, snake.'

'See you, sarge.'

The big cruiser snarled as Ben pulled back into the traffic lane and turned at the first corner. The city was on a system of neighbourhood police patrols, an attempt to avoid the anonymous patrolling that turned each car into a miniature search and destroy mission. The first night he sat on the stump beside his apartment, Lorne had sworn in surprise to see that the face peering from the curious patrol car was that of Ben Gresham, his squad leader during the ten months and nineteen days he had carried an M60 in War Zone C.

And that was the only past remaining to Lorne.

The back door of Jenkins' house banged shut on its spring. A few moments later heavy boots began scratching up the gravel of the common drive. Lorne's seat was an oak stump, three feet in diameter. Instead of trying to turn his head, he shifted his whole body around on the wood. Jenkins, a plumpish, half-bald man in his late sixties, lifted a pair of canned Budweisers. 'Must get thirsty out here, warm as it is.'

'It's always thirsty enough to drink good beer,' Lorne smiled. 'I'll share my stump with you.' They sipped for a time without speaking. Mrs Purefoy, Jenkins' widowed sister and a matronly Baptist, kept house for him. Lorne gathered that while she did not forbid her brother to drink an occasional beer, neither did she provide an encouragingly social atmosphere.

'I've seen you out here at 3 a.m.,' the older man said. 'What'll you do when the weather turns cold?'

'Freeze my butt for a while,' Lorne answered. He gestured his beer towards his dark apartment on the second floor of a house much like Jenkins'. 'Sit up there with the light on. Hell, there's lots of VA hospitals, I've *been* in lots of them. If North Carolina isn't warm enough, maybe they'd find me one in Florida.' He took another swallow and said, 'I just sleep better in the daytime, is all. Too many ghosts around at night.'

Jenkins turned quickly to make sure of the smile on the younger man's face. It flashed at his motion. 'Not quite that sort of ghost,' Lorne explained. 'The ones I bring with me . . .' And he kept his smile despite the sizzle of faces in the white fire sudden in his mind. The noise of popping, boiling flesh faded and he went on, 'There was something weird going on last night, though –' he glanced at his big Japanese wrist-watch – 'well, damn early this morning.'

'A Hallowe'en ghost with a white sheet?' Jenkins suggested.

'Umm, no, down at the church,' said Lorne, fumbling his cigarettes out. Jenkins shrugged refusal and the dart of butane flame ignited only one. 'The tower there was – I don't know, I looked at it and it seemed to be vibrating. No sound, though, and then a big red flash without any sound either. I thought it'd caught fire, but it was just a flash and everything was back to normal. Funny. You know how you hold your fingers over a flashlight and it comes through, kind of? Well, the flash was like that, only through a stone wall.'

'I never saw anything like that,' Jenkins agreed. 'Old church doesn't seem the worse for it, though. It'll be ready to fall down itself before the courts get all settled about who owns it, you know.'

'Umm?'

'Fellowship Baptist built a new church half a mile north of here, more parking and anyhow, it was going to cost more to repair that old firetrap than it would to build a new one.' Jenkins grinned. 'Mable hasn't missed a Sunday in forty years, so I heard all about it. The city bought the old lot for a boys' club or some such fool thing – I want to spit every time I think of my property taxes, I do – but it turns out the Rankins, that's who the street's named after too, they'd given the land way back before the Kaiser's War. Damn if some of them weren't still around to sue to get the lot back if it wasn't going to be a church any more. So that was last year, and it's like to be a few more before anybody puts money into tearing the old place down.'

'From the way it's boarded up and padlocked, I figured it must have been a reflection I saw,' Lorne admitted. 'But it looked funny enough,' he added sheepishly, 'that I took a walk down there last night.'

Jenkins shrugged and stood up. He had the fisherman's trick of dropping the pull tab into his beer before drinking any. Now it rattled in the bottom. 'Well,' he said, picking up Lorne's can as well, 'it's bed time for me, I suppose. You better get yourself off soon or the bugs'll carry you away.'

'Thanks for the beer and the company,' Lorne said. 'One of these nights I'll bring down an ice chest and we'll really tie one on.'

Lorne's ears followed the old man back, the sound of his boots friendly and even in the warm April darkness. A touch of breeze caught the wisteria hedge across the street and spread its sweetness, diluted, over Lorne. He ground out his cigarette and sat quietly, letting the vines breathe on him. Jenkins' garbage can scrunched open and one of the empties echoed into it. The other did not fall. 'What the hell?' Lorne wondered aloud. But there was something about the night, despite its urban innocence, that brought up memories from past years more strongly than ever before. In a little while Lorne began walking. He was still walking when dawn washed the fiery pictures from his mind and he returned to his apartment to find three police cars parked in the street.

The two other tenants stored their cars in the side yard of the apartment house. Lorne had stepped between them when he heard a woman scream, 'That's him! Don't let him get away!'

Lorne turned. White-haired Mrs Purefoy and a pair of uniformed policemen faced him from the porch of Jenkins' house. The younger man had his revolver half drawn. A third uniformed man, Ben, stepped quickly around from the back of the house. 'I'm not going anywhere but to bed,' Lorne said, spreading his empty hands. He began walking towards the others. 'Look, what's the matter?'

The oldest, heaviest of the policemen took the porch steps in a leap and approached Lorne at a barely-restrained trot. He had major's pips on his shoulder straps. 'Where have you been, snake?' Ben asked, but the major was between them instantly, growling, 'I'll handle this, Gresham. Mr Charles Lorne?'

'Yes,' Lorne whispered. His body flashed hot, as though the fat policeman were a fire, a towering sheet of orange rippling with the speckles of tracers cooking off . . .

'. . . and at any time during the questioning you may withdraw your consent and thereafter remain silent. Do you understand, Mr Lorne?'

'Yes.'

'Did you see Mr Jenkins tonight?'

'Uh-huh. He came out – when did you leave me, Ben? 10.30?' Lorne paused to light another cigarette. His flame wavered like the blade of a kris. 'We each drank a beer, shot the bull. That's all. What happened?'

'Where did you last seen Mr Jenkins?'

Lorne gestured. 'I was on the stump. He walked around the

back of the house – his house. I guess I could see him. Anyway, I heard him throw the cans in the trash and . . . that's all.'

'Both cans?' Ben broke in despite his commander's scowl.

'No, you're right – just one. And I didn't hear the door close. It's got a spring that slams it like a one-oh-five going off, usually. Look, what happened?'

There was a pause. Ben tugged at a corner of his moustache. Low sunlight sprayed Lorne through the trees. Standing, he looked taller than his six feet, a knobbly staff of a man in wheat jeans and a green-dyed T-shirt. The shirt had begun to disintegrate in the years since it was issued to him on the way to the war zone. The brace was baby-flesh pink. It made him look incongruously bull-necked, alien.

'He could have changed clothes,' suggested the young patrolman. He had holstered his weapon but continued to toy with the butt.

'He didn't,' Ben snapped, the signs of his temper obvious to Lorne if not to the other policemen. 'He's wearing now what he had on when I left him.'

'We'll take him around back,' the major suddenly decided. In convoy, Ben and the other, nervous, patrolman to either side of Lorne and the major bringing up the rear, they crossed into Jenkins' yard following the steep downslope. Mrs Purefoy stared from the porch. Beneath her a hydrangea bush graded its blooms red on the left, blue on the right, with the carefully-tended acidity of the soil. It was a mirror for her face, ruddy towards the sun and grey with fear in shadow.

'What's the problem?' Lorne wondered aloud as he viewed the back of the house. The trash can was open but upright, its lid lying on the smooth lawn beside it. Nearby was one of the Budweiser empties. The other lay alone on the bottom of the trash can. There was no sign of Jenkins himself.

Ben's square hand indicated an arc of spatters six to eight feet high, black against the white siding. 'They promised us a lab team but hell, it's blood, snake. You and me've seen enough to recognise it. Mrs Purefoy got up at four, didn't find her brother. I saw this when I checked and . . .' He let his voice trail off.

'No body?' Lorne asked. He had lighted a fresh cigarette. The gushing flames surrounded him.

'No.'

'And Jenkins weighs what? 220?' He laughed, a sound as thin as his wrists. 'You'd play hell proving a man with a broken neck ran off with him, wouldn't you?'

'Broke? Sure, we'll believe that!' gibed the nervous patrolman.

'You'll believe *me*, meatball!' Ben snarled. 'He broke it and he carried me out of a fucking burning shithook while our ammo cooked off. And by God –'

'Easy, sarge,' Lorne said quietly. 'If anybody needs shooting, I'll borrow a gun and do it myself.'

The major flashed his scowl from one man to the other. His sudden uncertainty was as obvious as the flag pin in his lapel: Lorne was now a veteran, not an ageing hippy.

'I'm an outpatient at the VA hospital,' Lorne said, seeing his chance to damp the fire. 'Something's fucking up some nerves and they're trying to do something about it there. Wish to hell they'd do it soon.'

'Gresham,' the major said, motioning Ben aside for a low-voiced exchange. The third policeman had gone red when Ben snapped at him. Now he was white, realising his mortality for the first time in his twenty-two years.

Lorne grinned at him. 'Hang loose, turtle. Neither Ben or me ever killed anybody who didn't need it worse than you do.'

The boy began to tremble.

'Mr Lorne,' the major said, his tone judicious but not hostile, 'we'll be getting in touch with you later. And if you recall anything, anything at all that may have bearing on Mr Jenkins' disappearance, call us at once.'

Lorne's hands nodded agreement. Ben winked as the lab van arrived, then turned away with the others.

Lorne's pain was less than usual, but his dreams awakened him in a sweat each time he dropped off to sleep. When at last he switched on the radio, the headline news was that three people besides Jenkins had disappeared during the night, all of them within five blocks of Lorne's apartment.

The air was very close, muffling the brilliance of the stars. It was Friday night and the roar of southbound traffic sounded from Donovan Avenue a block to the east. The three northbound lanes of Jones Street, the next one west of Rankin, were not yet as clotted with cars as they would be later at night, but headlights there were nervously darting through the houses and trees whenever Lorne turned on his stump to look. Rankin Street lay quietly between, lighted at alternate blocks by blue globes of mercury vapour. It was narrow, so that cars could not pass those parked along the kerb without slowing, easing a placid island surrounded by modern pressures.

But no one had disappeared to the east of Donovan or the west of Jones.

Lorne stubbed out his cigarette in the punky wood of the stump. It was riddled with termites and sometimes he pictured them, scrabbling through the darkness. He hated insects, hated especially the grubs and hidden things, the corpse-white termites . . . but he sat on the stump above them. A perversely objective part of Lorne's mind knew that if he could have sat in the heart of a furnace like the companions of Daniel, he would have done so.

From the blocky shade of the porch next door came the creak of springs: Mrs Purefoy, shifting her weight on the cushions of the old wing-back chair. In the early evening Lorne had caught her face staring at a parlour window, her muscles flat as wax. As the deeper darkness blurred and pooled, she had slipped out into its cover. Lorne felt her burning eyes, knowing that she would never forgive him for her brother's disappearance, not if it were proven that Jenkins had left by his own decision. Lorne had always been a sinner to her;

innocence would not change that.

Another cigarette. Someone else was watching. A passing car threw Lorne's angled shadow forward and across Jenkins' house. Lorne's guts clenched and his fingers crushed the unlit cigarette. *Light. Twelve men in a rice paddy when the captured flare bursts above them. The pop-pop-pop of a gun far off, and the splashes columning around Lt Burnes* –

'Christ!' Lorne shouted, standing with an immediacy that laced pain through his body. Something was terribly wrong in the night. The lights brought back memories, but they quenched the real threat that hid in the darkness. Lorne knew what he was feeling, *knew* that any instant a brown face would peer out of a spider hole behind an AK-47 or a mine would rip steel pellets down the trail . . .

He stopped, forcing himself to sit down again. If it was his time, there was nothing he could do about it. A fresh cigarette fitted between his lips automatically and the needle-bright lighter focused his eyes.

And the watcher was gone.

Something had poised to kill Lorne, and had then passed on without striking. It was as unnatural as if a wall collapsing on him had separated in mid-air to leave him unharmed. Lorne's arms were trembling, his cigarette tip an orange blur. When Ben's cruiser pulled in beside him, Lorne was at first unable to answer the other man's, 'Hey, snake.'

'Jesus, sarge,' Lorne whispered, smoke spurting from his mouth and nostrils. 'There's somebody out here and he's a *bad* fucker.'

Carrier noise blatted before the car radio rapped a series of numbers and street names. Ben knuckled his moustache until he was sure his own cruiser was not mentioned. 'Yeah, he's a bad one. Another one gone tonight, a little girl from three blocks down. Went to the store to trade six empties and a dime on a Coke. Christ, I *saw* her two hours ago, snake. The bottles we found, the kid we didn't . . . Seen any little girls?'

There was an upright shadow in front of Ben's radio: a riot

gun, clipped to the dashboard. 'Haven't seen anything but cars, sarge. Lots of police cars.'

'They've got an extra ten men on,' Ben agreed with a nod. 'We went over the old Baptist church a few minutes ago. Great TAC Squad work. Nothing. Damn locks were rusted shut.'

'Think the Baptists've taken up with baby sacrifice?' Lorne chuckled.

'Shit, there's five bodies somewhere. If the bastard's loading them in the back of a truck, you'd think he'd spread his pick-ups over a bit more of an area, wouldn't you?'

'Look, baby, anybody who packed Jenkins around on his back – I sure don't want to meet him.'

'Don't guess Jenkins did either,' Ben grunted. 'Or the others.'

'PD to D-5,' the radio interrupted.

Ben keyed his microphone. 'Go ahead.'

'10-25 Lt Cooper at Rankin and Duke.'

'10-4, 10-76,' Ben replied, starting to return the mike to its holder.

'D-5, acknowledge,' the receiver ordered testily.

'Goddam fucker!' Ben snarled, banging the instrument down. 'Sends just about half the fucking time!'

'Keep a low profile, sarge,' Lorne murmured, but even had he screamed his words would have been lost in the boom of exhaust as Ben cramped the car around in the street, the left wheels bumping over the far kerb. Then the accelerator flattened and the big car shot towards the rendezvous.

In Vietnam, Lorne had kept his death wish under control during shelling by digging in and keeping his head down. Now he stood and went inside to his room. After a time, he slept. If his dreams were bright and tortured, then they always were . . .

'Sure, you knew Jackson,' Ben explained, the poom-poom-poom of his engine a live thing in the night. 'He's the blond shit who . . . didn't believe you'd broken your neck. Yesterday morning.'

'Small loss, then,' Lorne grinned. 'But you watch your own ass, hear? If there's nobody out but cops, there's going to be more cops than just Jackson disappearing.'

'Cops and damned fools,' Ben grumbled. 'When I didn't see you out here on my first pass, I thought maybe you'd gotten sense enough to stay inside.'

'I was going to. Decided . . . oh, hell. What's the box score now?'

'Seven gone. Seven for sure,' the patrolman corrected himself. 'One got grabbed in the time he took to walk from his girl's front porch back to his car. That bastard's lucky, but he's crazy as hell if he thinks he'll stay that lucky.'

'He's crazy as hell,' Lorne agreed. A spring whispered from Jenkins' porch and Lorne bobbed the tip of his cigarette at the noise. 'She's not doing so good either. All last night she was staring at me, and now she's at it again.'

'Christ,' Ben muttered. 'Yeah, Major Hooseman talked to her this morning. You're about the baddest man ever, leading po' George into smoking and drinking and late hours before you killed him.'

'Never did get him to smoke,' Lorne said, lighting Ben's cigarette and another for himself. 'Say, did Jackson smoke?'

'Huh? No.' Ben frowned, staring at the closed passenger-side windows and their reflections of his instruments. 'Yeah, come to think, he did. But never in uniform, he had some sort of thing about that.'

'He sheered off last night when I lit a cigarette,' Lorne said. 'No, not Jackson – the other one. I just wondered . . .'

'You saw him?' Ben's voice was suddenly sharp, the hunter scenting prey.

Lorne shook his head. 'I just felt him. But he was there, baby.'

'Just like before they shot us down,' the policeman said quietly. 'You squeezing my arm and shouting over the damn engines "They're waiting for us, they're waiting for us!" And not a fucking thing I could do – I didn't order the assault and the Captain sure wasn't going to call it off because my machine-gunner said to. But you were right, snake.'

'The flames . . .' Lorne whispered, his eyes unfocused.

'And you're a dumb bastard to have done it, but you carried me out of them. It never helped us a bit that you knew when the shit was about to hit the fan. But you're a damn good man to have along when it does.'

Lorne's muscles trembled with memory. Then he stood and laughed into the night. 'You know, sarge, in twenty-seven years I've only found one job I was any good at. I didn't much like that one, and anyhow – the world doesn't seem to need killers.'

'They'll always need us, snake,' Ben said quietly. 'Sometimes they won't admit it.' Then, 'Well, I think I'll waste some more gas.'

'Sarge –' The word hung in the empty darkness. There was engine noise and the tyres hissing in the near distance and – nothing else. 'Sarge, Mrs Purefoy was on her porch a minute ago and she didn't go inside. But she's not there now.'

Ben's five-cell flashlight slid its narrow beam across the porch: the glider, the wing-back chair. On the far railing, a row of potted violets with a gap for the one now spilled on the boards as if by someone vaulting the rail but dragging one heel . . .

'Didn't hear it fall,' the policeman muttered, clacking open the car door. The dome light spilled a startling yellow pool across the two men. As it did so, white motion trembled half a block down Rankin Street.

'Fucker!' Ben said. 'He couldn't jump across the street, he threw something so it flashed.' Ben was back in the car.

Lorne squinted, furious at being blinded at the critical instant. 'Sarge, I'll swear to God he headed for the church.' Lorne strode stiffly around the front of the vehicle and got in on the passenger side.

'Mother-*fuck*!' the stocky policeman snarled, dropping the microphone that had three times failed to get him a response. He reached for the gear lever, looked suddenly at Lorne as the slender man unclipped the shotgun. 'Where d'ye think *you're* going?'

'With you.'

Ben slipped the transmission into Drive and hung a shrieking U-turn in the empty street. 'The first one's birdshot, the next four are double-ought buck,' he said flatly.

Lorne jacked the slide twice, chambering the first round and then shucking it out the ejector. It gleamed palely in the instrument light. 'Don't think we're going after birds,' he explained.

Ben twisted across the street and bounced over the driveway cut. The car slammed to a halt in the small lot behind and shielded by the bulk of the old church. It was a high, narrow building with two levels of boarded windows the length of the east and west sides; the square tower stood at the south end. At some time after its construction, the church had been faced with artificial stone. It was dingy, a grey mass in the night with a darkness about it that the night alone did not explain.

Ben slid out of the car. His flash touched the small door to the right of the tower. 'Nothing wrong with the padlock,' Lorne said. It was a formidable one, set in a patinated hasp to close the church against vandals and derelicts.

'They were all locked tight yesterday, too,' the patrolman said. 'He could still be getting in one of those windows. We'll see.' He turned to the trunk of the car and opened it, holding his flashlight in the crook of his arm so his right hand could be free for his drawn revolver.

Lorne's quick eyes scanned the wall above them. He bent back at the waist instead of tilting his head alone. 'Got the key?' he asked.

The stocky man chuckled, raising a pair of folding shovels, army surplus entrenching tools. 'Keep that corn-sheller ready,' he directed, holstering his own weapon. He locked the blade

of one shovel at 90° to the shaft and set it on top of the padlock.
The other, still folded, cracked loudly against the head of the
first and popped the lock open neatly. 'Field expedients, snake,'
Ben laughed. 'If we don't find anything, we can just shut the
place up again and nobody will know the difference.'

He tossed the shovels aside and swung open the door. The
air that puffed out had the expected mustiness of a long-closed
structure with a sweetish overtone that neither man could
have identified. Lorne glanced around the outside once more,
then followed the patrolman within. The flames in his mind
were very close.

'Looks about like it did last night,' Ben said.

'And last year, I'd guess.' The wavering oval of the flashlight
picked over the floor. The hardwood was warping, pocked at
frequent intervals by holes.

'They unbolted the old pews when they moved,' Ben
explained. 'Took the stained glass too, since the place was
going to be torn down.'

The nave was a single narrow room running from the
chancel in the north to the tower which had held the organ
pipes and, above, the chimes. The main entrance was by a side
aisle, through double doors in the middle of the west wall.
The interior looked a gutted ruin.

'You checked the whole building?' Lorne asked. The pulpit
had been ripped away. The chancel rail remained though half-
splintered, apparently to pass the organ and altar. Fragments
of wood, crumpled boxes, and glass littered the big room.

'The main part. We didn't have the key to the tower and the
major didn't want to bust in.' Ben took another step into the
nave and kicked at a stack of old bulletins.

White heat, white fire – 'Ben, did you check the ceiling when
you were here last night?'

'Huh?' The narrow Gothic vault was blackness forty feet
above the ground. Ben's flashlight knifed upward across
painted plaster to the ribbed and panelled ceiling that sloped
to the main beam. And – 'Jesus!'

A large cocoon was tight against the roof peak. It shimmered palely azure, but the powerful light thrust through to the human outline within. Long shadows quivered on the wood, magnifying the trembling of the policeman's wrist as the beam moved from the cocoon to another beside it, to the third –

'Seven of the fuckers!' Ben cried, taking another step and slashing the light to the near end of the room where the south wall closed the inverted V of the ceiling. Above the door to the tower was the baize screen of the pipe loft. The cloth fluttered behind Mrs Purefoy, who stood stiffly upright twenty feet in the air. Her face was locked in horror, framed by her tousled white hair. Both arms were slightly extended but were stone-rigid within the lace-fringed sleeves of her dress.

'She –' Lorne began, but as he spoke and Ben's hand fell to the butt of his revolver, Mrs Purefoy began to fall, tilting a little in a rustle of skirts. Beneath the crumpled edge of the baize curtain, spiked on the beam of Ben's flashlight, gleamed the head and foreclaws of what had been clutching the woman.

The eyes glared like six-inch opals, fierce and hot in a dead white exoskeleton. The foreclaws clicked sideways. As though they had cocked a spring, the whole flat torso shot down at Ben.

An inch long and scuttling under a rock it might have passed for a scorpion, but this lunging monster was six feet long without counting the length of the tail arced back across its body. Flashing legs, flashing body armour, and the fluid-jewelled sting that winked as Lorne's finger twitched in its killer's reflex –

Lorne's body screamed at the recoil of the heavy charge. The creature spun as if kicked in mid-air, smashing into the floor a yard from Ben instead of on top of the policeman. The revolver blasted, a huge yellow bottle-shape flaring from the muzzle. The bullet ripped away a window shutter because a six-inch pincer had locked Ben's wrist. The creature reared onto the back two pairs of its eight jointed legs. Lorne stepped sideways for a clear shot, the slide of his weapon slick-snacking another round into the chamber. On the creature's white belly was a smeared, multibrancate star – the load of buckshot had ricocheted off, leaving a trail like wax on glass.

Ben clubbed his flashlight. It cracked harmlessly between the glowing eyes and sprang from his hand. The other claw flashed to Ben's face and trapped it, not crushingly but hard enough to immobilise and start blood-trails down both cheeks. The blades of the pincer ran from nose to hairline on each side.

Lorne thrust his shotgun over Ben's right shoulder and fired point blank. The creature rocked back, jerking a scream from the policeman as the claws tightened. The lead struck the huge left eye and splashed away, dulling the opal shine. The flashlight still glaring from the floor behind the creature silhouetted its sectioned tail as it arched above the policeman's head. The armed tip plunged into the base of his neck. Ben stiffened.

Lorne shouted and emptied his shotgun. The second dense red bloom caught like a strobe light the dotted line of blood droplets joining Ben's neck to the withdrawn injector. A claw seized Lorne's waist in the rolling echo of the shotgun blasts. His gunbutt cracked on the creature's armour, steel sparking as it slid off. The extending pincer brushed the shotgun aside and clamped over Lorne's face, half-shielding from him the sight of the rising sting.

Then it smashed on Lorne's neck brace, and darkness exploded over him in a flare of coruscant pain.

The oozing ruin of Mrs Purefoy's face stared at Lorne through its remaining eye when he awoke. Everything swam in blue darkness except for one bright blur. He blinked and the blur suddenly resolved into a street-light glaring up through a shattered board. Lorne's lungs burned and his stiffness seemed more than even unconsciousness and the pain skidding through his nerve paths could explain. He moved his arm and something clung to its surface; the world quivered.

Lorne was hanging from the roof of the church in a thin, transparent sheath. Mrs Purefoy was a yard away, multiple wrappings shrouding her corpse more completely. With a strength not far from panic, Lorne forced his right fist into the bubble around him. The material, extruded in broad swathes by the creature rather than as a loom of threads, sagged but did not tear. The clear azure turned milky under stress and sucked in around Lorne's wrist.

He withdrew his hand. The membrane passed some oxygen but not enough for an active man. Lorne's hands patted the outside of his pockets finding, as he had expected, nothing with a sharp edge. He had not recently bitten off his thumbnails. Thrusting against the fire in his chest, he brought his left hand in front of his body. With a fold of the cocoon between each thumb and index finger, he thrust his hands apart. A rip started in the white opacity beneath his right thumb. Air, clean and cool, jetted in.

'Oh, Jesus,' Lorne muttered, even the pain in his body forgotten as he widened the tear upwards to his face. The cocoon was bobbing on a short lead, rotating as the rip changed its balance. Lorne could see that he had become ninth in the line of hanging bodies, saved from their paralysis by the chance of his neck brace. Ben, his face blurred by the membrane holding him next to Lorne, had been less fortunate.

Ten yards from where Lorne hung and twenty feet below the roof beam, the baize curtain of the pipe loft twitched. Lorne froze in fearful immobility.

The creature had been able to leap the width of a street carrying the weight of an adult; its strength must be as awesome as was the rigidity of its armour. Whether or not it could drive its sting through Lorne's brace, it could assuredly rip him to collops if it realised he was awake.

The curtain moved again, the narrow ivory tip of a pincer lifting it slightly. The creature was watching Lorne.

Ben carried three armour-piercing rounds in his ·357 magnum for punching through car doors. Lorne tried to remember whether the revolver had remained in Ben's hand as he fell. There was no image of that in Lorne's mind, only the torch-like muzzle blasts of his own shotgun. Slim as it was, his only hope was that the jacketed bullets would penetrate the creature's exoskeleton though the soft buckshot had not.

Lorne twisted his upper torso out of the hole for a closer look at Ben, making his own cocoon rock angrily. The baize lifted further. The street-light lay across it in a pale band. Why didn't the creature scuttle out to finish the business?

Brief motion waked a flash of scintillant colour from the pipe loft. The curtain flapped closed as if a volley of shots had ripped through it. Lorne recognised the reflex: the panic of a spider when a stick thrusts through its web. Not an object, though; the light itself, weak as it was, had slapped the creature back. Ben's bright flashlight had not stopped it when necessity drove, but the monster must have felt pain at human levels of illumination. Its eyes were adapted to starlight or the glow of a sun immeasurably fainter than that of Earth. 'Where did you come from, you bastard?' Lorne whispered.

Light. It gave him an idea and he fumbled out his butane lighter, adjusting it to a maximum flame. The sheathes were relatively thin over the victims' faces to aid transpiration. At the waist, though, where a bulge showed Ben's arm locked to his torso, the membrane was thick enough to be opaque in the dim light. Lorne bent dangerously over, cursing the stiffness of his neck brace. Holding the inch-high jet close, he tried to peer through Ben's cocoon. Unexpectedly the fabric gave a little and Lorne bobbed forward, bringing the flame in contact with the material sheathing Ben.

The membrane sputtered, kissing Lorne's hand painfully. He jerked back and the lighter flicked away. It dropped, cold and silent until it cracked on the floor forty feet below. Despite the pattern of light over it, the curtain to the loft was shifting again. Lorne cursed in terror.

A line of green fire sizzled up the side of Ben's cocoon from the point at which the flame had touched it. The material across his face flared. The policeman gave no sign of feeling his skin curl away. The revolver in his hand winked green.

Lorne screamed. His own flexible prison lurched and sagged like heated polyethylene. Ben was wrapped in a cancerous hell that roared and heaved against the roof-beams as a live thing. Green tongues licked yellow-orange flames from the dry wood as well. Lorne's cocoon and that to the other side of Ben were deforming in the furnace heat. Another lurch and Lorne had slipped twenty feet, still gripped around the waist in a sack of blue membrane. He was gyrating like a top. The loft curtain had twitched higher each time it spun past his vision.

The bottom of Ben's cocoon burned away and he plunged past Lorne, face upward and still afire. Bone crunched as he hit. The body rebounded a few inches to fall again on its face. The roar of the flames muffled Lorne's wail of rage. His own elongated capsule began to flow. Flames grasped at Lorne's support. Before they could touch the sheathing, the membrane pulled a last few inches and snapped like an overstretched rubber band. The impact of the floor smashed Lorne's jaw against his neck brace, grinding each tortured vertebra against the next. He did not lose consciousness, but the shock paralysed him momentarily as thoroughly as the creature's sting could have done.

Bathed in green light and the orange of the blazing roof panels, the scorpion thing thrust its thorax into the nave. Its walking legs gripped the flat surface, dimpling the plaster. The creature turned upward towards the fire, three more cocoons alight and their hungry flames lapping across the beams. Then, parti-coloured by the illumination, its legs shifted and the opal eyes trained on Lorne. The light must be torture to it, muffling in indecision its responses, but it was about to act.

A small form wrapped in a flaming shroud dropped to thump the floor beside Lorne. His arms would move again. He used them to strip the remaining sheathing from his legs. It clung as the heat of the burning corpse began to melt the material. Something writhed from a crackling tumour on the child's neck. The thing was finger-long and seemed to paw the air with a score of tiny legs; its opalescent eyes proved its parentage. The creature brought more than paralysis to its victims: it was a gravid female.

Green flame touched the larva. It burst in a postular smear.

The adult went mad. Its legs shot it almost the length of the nave to rebound from a sidewall in a cloud of plaster. The creature's horizontally-flattened tail ruddered it instinctively short of the fire as it leapt upward to the roof peak. It clung there in pale horror against the wood, eyes on the advancing flames. Three more bodies fell, splashing like ginkgo fruits.

Lorne staggered upright. The fire hammered down at him without bringing pain. His body had no feeling whatever. Ben's hair had burned. His neck and scalp were black where skin remained, red where it had cracked open to the muscle beneath. The marbled background showed clearly the tiny, pallid hatchling trying to twist across it.

Lorne's toe brushed the larva onto the floor. His boot heel struck it, struck again and twisted. Purulent ichor spurted between the leather and the boards. Lorne knelt. In one motion he swung Ben across his shoulders and stood, just as he had after their helicopter had nosed into the trees and exploded. Logic had been burned out of Lorne's mind, leaving only a memory of friendship. He did not look up. As his mechanical steps took him and his burden through the door they had entered, a shadow wavered across them. The creature had sprung back into the loft.

Lorne stumbled to his knees in the parking lot. The church had been rotten and dry. Orange flames fluffed through the roof in several places, thrusting corkscrews of sparks into the night sky. Twelve feet of roof slates thundered into the nave. Flame spewed up like a secondary explosion. There were sirens in the night.

Without warning, the east façade of the tower collapsed into the parking lot. Head-sized chunks of Tennessee-stone smashed at the patrol car, one of them missing Lorne by inches. He looked up, blank-eyed, his hands lightly touching the corpse of his friend. Of its own volition, the right hand traced down Ben's shoulder to the raw flesh of his elbow. The tower stairs spiralled out of the dust and rubble, laid bare to the steel framework when the wall fell. On the sagging floor of the pipe loft rested a machine like no other thing on Earth, and the creature was inside it. Tubes of silvery metal rose cradleform from a base of similar metal. The interstices were not filled with anything material, but the atmosphere seemed to shiver, blurring the creature's outline.

And Lorne's hand was unwrapping Ben's stiff fingers from the grips of his revolver.

Lorne stood again, his left hand locking his right on the butt of the big magnum. He was familiar with the weapon: it was the one Ben had carried in Nam, the same tool he had used for five of his thirteen kills. It would kill again tonight.

Even in the soaring holocaust the sharp crack of Lorne's shot was audible. Lorne's forearms rocked up as a unit with the recoiling handgun. The creature lurched sideways to touch the shimmering construct around it. A red surface discharge rippled across the exoskeleton from the point of contact. Lorne fired again. He could see the armour dull at his point of aim in the centre of the thorax. Again the creature jumped. Neither bullet had penetrated, but the splashing lead of the second cut an upright from the machine. The creature spun, extending previously-unglimpsed tendrils from the region of its mouth parts. They flickered over a control plate in the base. Machinery chimed in response.

The shivering quickened. The machine itself and the thing it enclosed seemed to fade. Lorne thumb-cocked the magnum, lowered the red vertical of the front sight until it was even with the rear notch; the creature was a white blur beyond them. The gun bucked back hard when he squeezed; the muzzle blast was sharper, flatter, than before. The first of the armour-piercing bullets hit the creature between the paired tendrils.

The exoskeleton surrounding them shattered like safety glass struck by a brick.

The creature straightened in silent agony, rising onto its hind legs with its tail lying rigidly against its back. Its ovipositor was fully extended, thumb-thick and six inches long.

'Was it fun to kill them, bug?' Lorne screamed. 'Was it as much fun as this is?' His fourth shot slammed, dimpling a belly plate which then burst outward in an ugly gush of fluids. The creature's members clamped tightly about its spasming thorax. The tail lashed the uprights in red spurts. The machine was fading and the torn panelling of the loft was beginning to show through the dying creature's body.

There was one shot left in the cylinder and Lorne steadied his sights on the control plate. He had already begun taking up the last pressure when he stopped and lowered the muzzle. No, let it go home, whatever place or time that might be. Let its fellows see that Earth was not their hunting ground alone. And if they came back anyway – *if they only would*!

There was a flash as penetrating as the first microsecond of a nuclear blast. The implosion dragged Lorne off his feet and sucked in the flames so suddenly that all sound seemed frozen. Then both sidewalls collapsed into the nave and the ruins of the tower twisted down on top of them. In the last instant, the pipe loft was empty of all but memory.

A fire truck picked its way through the rubble in the parking lot. Its headlights flooded across the figure of a sandy-haired man wearing scorched clothing and a neck brace. He was kneeling beside a body, and the tears were bright on his face.

The Petey Car

by

MANLY WADE WELLMAN

Manly Wade Wellman (1903–) is one of the most careful and convincing writers to have contributed to the finest of horror magazines, Weird Tales. *Before he began to write full-time his career was enviably varied (harvest hand, cowboy, bouncer, newspaperman); his writing reads like that of a man who has met and understood many kinds of people. Like David Drake (and Karl Wagner, the fantasy writer) he lives in Chapel Hill; there must be something in the air.*

Among his sixty-six books or more are two superb collections of macabre stories: Who Fears The Devil *and* Worse Things Waiting. *His tales chill the more deeply for the quietness of their telling; he credits their believability to 'the great and understanding help of a great and understanding editor' – Farnsworth Wright, of* Weird Tales. *Here is the kind of tale of terror that made* Weird Tales *inimitable.*

Old Mr Freddy Chunn's Petey car was the only competition when City Cab came into town, but City Cab didn't want even that much, and killed it off by sort of killing old Mr Freddy off.

For long years the Petey car had carried folks over town and up to mountain homes round about, for just reasonable charges. Mr Freddy had glasses and a hangdown white moustache, and lived in a little shack of a house, the last one on Indian Rock Street. When his wife died, Mr Freddy said, 'This here Petey car's my only family I've got left now. Him and me understands one another. If you ain't sure where you want to ride, Petey's sure,' and then he'd take you whatever place you called for. Folks said the Petey car must be near about as old as Mr Freddy. Nobody even rightly knew what make it had been to start out, he'd repaired it so much – parts out of old wrecks and sometimes new parts he'd hammered out himself, at the mule shoe shop. But it ran right well.

Then the county seat got to be a resort town, with summer homes all over, and up the slopes on Copper Knob and Fox Laurel and even towards Yandro. The new Chamber of Commerce dammed up Worley's Creek to make a swimming beach. A riding stable came in, and two golf courses where the ground was flat enough, and auto courts and gift shops and things like that. And finally City Cab, when the county seat, only three thousand souls in winter, got to be twenty thousand in summer, wearing sports clothes and having cocktail parties.

J. J. Slesinger owned City Cab. He was heavy-set, bald headed and red faced and had about twenty sharp suits. He said that Mr Freddy had to go. 'This is my town,' he said, as if he'd bought it and could show you the receipt.

But old-timers still rode with Mr Freddy, and their young folks too, for he was jolly and knew songs and stories. Pretty, black-haired Lee Lonnie Burnett, who was cashier at Aunt Bush's Café, was special with him, for they were someway cousins. He'd carry her home from work. A couple of times when young Joe Patch rode along, so much in love with Lee Lonnie he couldn't talk, Mr Freddy didn't even charge them when he set them down where Lee Lonnie lived with Aunt Bush on Sockman Road.

So J. J. Slesinger sat down in his back office with Rudd Stowe and said, 'Put that old gaffer out of the cab business, and you'll be better off here than you were when you spent your time standing in front of the pool hall in your home town.'

'Leave it to me, Chief,' said Rudd, big as a bear and not a quarter as kind in the face. His hair was scaldy yellow and up the side of his jaw ran a thin scar. 'Give me two-three weeks,' said Rudd, winking a pale blue eye and smiling with flat white teeth.

That night he let the air out of the Petey car's tyres, and Mr Freddy wheezed from pumping them up. Next night, Rudd put sugar lumps in the petrol tank so it had to be drained and the lines blown out. He changed his voice and phoned Mr Freddy to come get somebody way high up on Sixkiller Ridge late at night in the rain, and nobody was there. The way down was scary to roll. Mr Freddy said the Petey car more or less drove itself down.

'I named it for a horse I used to ride,' he said in Aunt Bush's Café. 'Once I got snowed in at a banjo-picking and I gave that Petey horse his head and he got me home. I can near about do that with my Petey car, but it was a long drive for nothing.'

'Have some of this pie with your coffee, Cousin Freddy,' said Lee Lonnie Burnett. 'Who'd be common enough to trick you like that?'

Rudd Stowe and the City Cab bookkeeper laughed in their booth, over hamburgers and the bottle they'd fetched in.

Mr Freddy hadn't taken in much money the best of times and he was taking in less, now the worse times had come. When old friends would bid him to supper, he appreciated it. Meanwhile, Rudd kept playing his tricks till the last one, fourth of July night, when Mr Freddy drove to where the bus was coming in, hoping he could pick up a fare.

The Petey car slowed to roll into the kerb beside the new front of the bus station, and nobody saw Rudd fling a bunch of fire-crackers up on the hood to blast off in a loud rattle right against the windshield. Mr Freddy thought the motor was blowing up somehow, and next moment he'd smashed into the station. The Petey car was no more than dinted, but the glass windows of the station went to pieces, and everybody jumped out to yell that it was hundreds of dollars in damages for Mr Freddy to pay.

How would he pay it? He'd never saved anything. He'd been just getting by, and lately not even that. Judge Spence wasn't taking rent for that little place he lived on Indian Rock Street. His clothes were old. All he might raise money on were a big gold watch and the Petey car, not worth fifty dollars together. He heard what they yelled at him and said yes, yes, yes, all right, and drove off alone.

He headed up Indian Rock Street, past his place that was the last one there, drove in the dark between bunchy-leaved trees where sometimes you thought faces showed in the shadows, to the end of the street, the big rock where once the Indians had worshipped gods that mustn't be let come up out of the ground where they lived. Next day somebody found him there, with his head down on his crossed arms on the wheel. Rudd Stowe's tricks had got Mr Freddy all the way out of competition with City Cab. He was dead.

His friends mourned him. Judge Spence bought the watch and gave it to Lee Lonnie Burnett. J. J. Slesinger bid highest for the Petey car and had Rudd Stowe into the back office for another talk.

'Here's how I'll pay you off,' said J. J. Slesinger. 'That old hack will be publicity for us. Some of these country fools like to ride in it for old time's sake. So you drive it, and for the time being you can keep whatever fares you get. You should do right well, good-looking and smart spoken like you are. And later on, we just might need your tricks again one of these days.'

So Rudd went out in the Petey car, with a City Cab sign on the door, doing what seemed all right for himself.

The older town folks did still want to ride the Petey car. Rudd shone at his job, smiling, saying yessum, yessir, big hands on the wheel, driving you where you wanted. And some of the summer people, pretty ladies like Mrs Rachel Lindsey

Walker and Mrs C. C. Van Huyl, said how bright and clever Rudd was, how he'd look all right in a white jacket at their parties, and tipped him big along with his fare. He began to say, 'I vow, them kind pays me to take their money. I've got the only game in town, with the cream on top of the jam.'

He spoke well of the Petey car, too. 'You never seen the like, how it's geared and wired,' he told Lee Lonnie at the café. 'That old Freddy fellow knowed what he was doing. It's a pleasure to drive it,' and he grinned at her. 'It would be a double pleasure if you'd let me drive you home.'

'I'm going home with Joe Patch,' she said, making change.

'That'll be going home with nothing at all,' Rudd laughed, and then he laughed harder when Joe Patch glittered an eye at him from down the counter. But when he went out and drove away, the motor made a deep, rough, growling sound for a block or so, like a mean animal of some sort. Rudd couldn't figure out why.

But mostly, he made good runs. He liked the way the Petey car took tall hills with out-of-town fares, and how the tyres stood up. He gave that car only high test petrol, and oiled it and greased it himself. But one night, when he was driving after work to a backroom crap game, it died. He cranked the starter pedal and it died again, and he had to walk four blocks to the game and four blocks back. When he wanted to go home, the car drove as lovely as a music box.

'God damn this old heap's time,' said Rudd, 'I've got a mind to pull out the whole engine and put in another.' But it was running so sweetly by then, and next morning too, he left things the way they were.

Some of the town girls, and the summer girls too, got pitching to Rudd. He was good at pitching back. But he figured to do something about Lee Lonnie. She was just playing hard to get, he told the boys at City Cab garage. That kind of girl usually turned out easiest to get. Joe Patch's time wouldn't be any trouble to beat.

One night he started driving along the street beside Joe and Lee Lonnie as they left the café. He honked and hoorawed at them. Two or three folks laughed, and a couple of others said, 'Well, I never.' But when Joe and Lee Lonnie turned a corner, the Petey car didn't follow, even when Rudd swung hard on the wheel. It just went across the street and conked out on the other side. He tried to start it, tried again, then got out and looked under the hood. Finally he got back in and cranked one more time. The Petey car started up fine, but by then Joe and Lee Lonnie were gone off he didn't know where.

'I vow,' said Rudd out loud through his teeth, 'it's like as if this here old wreck's trying to make a fool of me.'

Then's when a thin, nasty voice spoke one word close to his ear:

Trying?

'Who said that?' yelled Rudd, looking out this window and that. But nobody was passing anywhere near him. He was all alone right there, him and the Petey car and whatever had said the word. He drove off to answer a call. He felt shaken awhile, and he was shaken worse that night when he got hit for twenty-two dollars in the crap game. He wondered if his luck was gone bad for sure.

Next day, cruising Main Street, he heard a bothersome noise in the car, *tut-tut-tut*, and he headed for the garage and had the wheels off to look at the bearings. Nothing wrong with them. 'Come drive this thing a few blocks and see how you think she runs,' he asked Oaty Crocker, and Oaty got in with him and took the wheel. The Petey car purred and handled for a prize, all the way round the block.

'She runs better than the one I'm hacking with, Rudd,' said Oaty, and Rudd felt better. Out he went again and carried a fare, then another, and no trouble. But when he drove back from the second trip, there was a whine in things, like a stormy wind somewhere. Rudd didn't like it at all.

Rudd had lived low, but he wasn't thick in the head. He didn't take long to find out that these bothers never happened when he had a passenger; only when he was by himself in the Petey car. He went to see J. J. Slesinger in the back office and asked if he could have another cab.

'What's wrong with the one you have and the money I let you keep?' J. J. Slesinger wanted him to say.

'Well, it runs funny. Sometimes I wonder if it ain't haunted.'

'Haunted.' A hard sort of grin with that. 'I've overheard you talking some crazy stuff of that sort. If you keep on with that talk, you could hurt me and you both.'

'How you mean, Chief?' asked Rudd.

'Some of these old branch-head dwellers round about here believe in hauntings. But they figure a ghost that won't rest easy has reasons to be restless, and that might start up questions about the sad death of old Freddy Chunn.' J. J. Slesinger leaned across the desk. 'I got you here because I thought you could keep your trap shut and be satisfied with things, more or less.'

'Chief, I just don't want to drive that old car no more,' Rudd said with a shake in his voice. 'Maybe I ought to just quit and go back where I come from.'

'Do that, Rudd.' J. J. Slesinger grinned harder. 'Go back where you came from, and there'll be a word from me going back to the same place, to a couple of guys I know there. Because I don't want you in some other town, maybe running off at the mouth about things. I'm a good business man, Rudd, spreading out. I know people to handle my out-of-town business if it needs handling. All right, do you still want to leave?'

Rudd swallowed hard. 'No, sir. I'll stick.'

'That's my boy. Maybe there'll be a couple of other special little things come up one of these days, that will suit your talents. Meanwhile, keep on driving that car, and let's not hear any more of your spooky stories.'

Rudd went back out in the Petey car, and again he seemed to hear something like a word by that thin voice he'd heard before:

Okay...

He didn't ask who said it this time. He didn't want to know.

At supper time that night, Rudd drove over to talk to Jen Bate, hoping he wasn't being a fool to do it.

Jen was one of the folks who'd caught on with the resort crowd. She used to have the name of being a devilish witch woman with some, but the summer people weren't scared, they thought it was fun to pay her money to tell them strange things. She'd say what was in their futures or how to play the stock market. When she told Mrs Van Huyl to look in her last year's purse and find the bracelet she'd thought was lost or stolen, her business picked up. She even got hired to come to parties, like a show. Rudd came into her front room, where the windows were hung over with black velvet and on the carve-legged table stood a glass bowl with a light from somewhere reflected in it to glimmer his eyes, and Jen bade him sit down across from her.

She was maybe forty, with a long pale face and dark hair in two snaky braids on her shoulders, and round her neck a chain with a little skull-shaped thing on it. She asked for ten dollars before he could even say what he was after, and he paid it. Then, feeling more like a fool yet, he told her all about the car trouble.

'Yes,' said Jen when he had finished, 'and why do you bring that business here?'

'I want to know what to believe.'

'Give me ten dollars more.'

He gave it to her, and she looked into the glass bowl. Then she picked up a big conch shell and set it to her ear. She looked at Rudd, and her dark, shining eyes seemed to see down to his bones. Finally:

'I heard a voice,' she said.

'Was it,' and he licked his dry lips. 'Was it that old Freddy Chunn?'

'Why do you ask?'

He flung out his big hands, as if he begged. 'I never killed him. Never even touched him.'

'No, you just devilled him to death. Pressured him till he was pressed to death.'

'Was it him you heard talk?' asked Rudd again.

'No,' she said, drawing it out slowly. 'From all I can tell you, he's at rest. Anyway, you already have the answer.'

'I don't think I understand you.'

'The car itself,' she told him. 'That's an unusual car, son.'

'Yessum, it sure enough is. Been worked over so much it's completely different from what it started out.'

Jen's eyes slid all over him. 'Mr Freddy used to be sort of good to me when some others spoke against me,' she said. 'Used to carry me places when I didn't have as much money as I've got now. I was grateful for that help, and I gave help to him.'

'Did he ask you for witch help?' said Rudd, feeling cold down his back.

'He didn't hold with such things, so I never told him what I did. When his car would run down, I'd say a few words over my shoulder so he couldn't hear. Ran a few spells. You look funny, son. I don't think you believe me.'

'I believe you,' he hastened to say. 'I'm trying to figure. A car's just a machine.'

'Yes, and this is the machine age, and that's been going on for ever since the first men and women,' she said.

'Is that right?' Rudd wondered. 'I thought first the stone age –'

'You don't understand, son.' That sounded scornful on her mouth. 'The stone age was part of the machine age. A machine's anything a man makes to help him. The machine age goes back to when man first flung rocks at birds, or made stone knives to stab with, or spears to make his arm longer to stab with the knife. Or when he first used a pole to pry up a heavy weight. Or when he got to using fire and making clothes. It's gone on from how many hundreds of thousand years we can't count. And it's got to where machines, the things we make, sometimes run us.'

'I've heard tell of that,' Rudd put in. 'Machines that can add and subtract and divide quicker than men, all like that.'

'Everything, I tell you,' said Jen. 'Man is nothing without his own makings. Where'd you be without shoes or clothes? How'd you kill a rabbit without a gun, or catch a fish without a hook and line? How'd you live without driving that car old Mr Freddy used to call Petey? And you tell me it drives itself sometimes. Takes over from you. Cars can do that. Look how many folks would starve without a car to carry them two blocks to the grocery store.'

'But no car should be able to talk,' Rudd argued.

'Phonographs can talk,' she reminded him.

'This ain't no phonograph, it's a car. That's different.'

'It sure is,' she agreed. 'A sure enough different car. I'd guess that you hear it talking because it does talk. I don't reckon that Petey car likes you, son.'

'There may be a lot in what you say,' he had to admit. 'A car does more for one man than another. Sometimes a car will just lay down on a man, like a mean mule.'

'Right, son, if the mule feels mean about the man. And you sound as if that old car feels mean towards you.'

Rudd chewed his tongue to think. Finally: 'Well, if you put a spell on it to make it that sort of car, you could take the spell off again.'

'I can tell you just one way to make that car right with you, and it'll cost you a hundred dollars.'

His blue eyes opened up. He felt in his pocket. 'I ain't got but seventy-four.'

'Well, fork it over.'

He dug out all the money he had, and she counted it and put it away.

'Your answer is Lee Lonnie Burnett,' she told Rudd.

'How come?'

'That car knows her. She and Mr Freddy were kinfolks. She rode with him and talked to him. She called that car by its Petey name. She knows it, and it knows her.'

Rudd wondered how it all sounded so right, when it was like a crazy story out of a crazy book.

'You'd like to leave out of that car and go away,' Jen was saying. 'Your boss has you scared to do that. So you'll have to make Lee Lonnie help you, get you right with the car. That's all for now, son, and come back when you think you need me again.'

Going out, he felt that the Petey car had its headlights sort of turned as if they watched him. He got in and started, and deep in the engine came a whining noise for just a moment. He drove to Aunt Bush's Café and went in and sat at the counter. 'Lee Lonnie,' he said, 'I want to see you.'

'You see me,' she said, not very friendly.

'This is just a small town, and us two ought to get along,' he tried to say. 'If I ever spoke out of turn, I want to get back in turn. What if I said you could ride in that old cab the way you used to, that I'd come fetch you home every night and charge you nothing?'

'I don't know what he's leading up to, Lee Lonnie,' said Aunt Bush, from up the counter where she was clearing away dishes. 'But I wouldn't let him lead me there if I was you.'

'I don't mean her no harm,' Rudd said, and went on out. He carried a couple of fares, and the Petey car went all right with them, but when he was alone between carrying the two he thought there was a laugh in the empty car with him. From beside him, or from the back seat. Something laughed, and it wasn't a friendly laugh.

He drove off with a young couple, then an old couple. The Petey car kept running like a dream with passengers. But when he was alone in it, there'd be buckings as if the fuel line was clogged, there was a soft hiss like steam though the cooling system was all right, and a fog on the windshield that went away before he could start the wipers. That Petey car was having fun with him – or else it was being dead serious. It was getting worse all the time, every day, every hour. Just now it swerved, all of itself, almost in front of a big glare-lighted truck that honked him angrily out of its way, just inches out.

He stopped in front of the movie theatre, shaking all over, till a bunch of kids came out and rode with him up to one of the summer cottages high up Fox Laurel. He was glad to take them back there, but he wished he didn't have to come down. There's a long drop on the right of the road, and the Petey car ran to within inches of the edge, seemed to look down while Rudd whimpered inside. Back in town, not sure what luck got him there, he put on the brakes at Aunt Bush's Café again. It was near closing time.

'Lee Lonnie,' he said when he got to the counter, 'I've purely got to see you.'

'You've seen me once tonight,' she said. 'That ought to be enough for you. It was enough for me.'

'But this is important to me,' he fairly begged.

'No,' she said. 'Nothing about me should concern you in the least.'

'Listen,' he tried desperately, 'maybe I started out all wrong with you –'

'I won't quarrel with you on that,' she said.

'Leave her alone,' said Aunt Bush, coming up behind him. 'If you don't want anything to eat, get out of here, or I'll call the law to help you find the way.'

He went out, feeling sick to the roots of his toes. He got back in the Petey car, but he didn't touch the starter. He waited, trying to think of what to say when it was time to say it. He wore his way through a quarter of an hour of time, slow and miserable as wearing through six feet of ice. At last Lee Lonnie came out, alone.

'Lee Lonnie!' he called to her, as if he was drowning and

only she could save him. 'Lee Lonnie, get in with me, let me drive you home and talk to you!'

She headed along the walk, putting her chin up, not speaking. He started the car and caught up. He mashed down the brake and went into park and jumped out. Catching her slim wrist in his big hand, he dragged her to the car.

'I'm not going to hurt you,' he kept saying. 'I've got to have your help. Let me tell you about it, you'll see how it is –'

She screamed as he slammed her into the car and then ran around to jump in himself and start up before she could get out again. She screamed louder. Folks came running along the walk. He speeded up to get away from them.

'I just want you to listen,' he tried to tell her, but Lee Lonnie wasn't listening. She was screaming. 'Help!' she screamed. 'Help me! Get me away from him!'

'I'm willing to pay you,' Rudd started to say, then remembered he'd given Jen Bate all his money. They'd come to a stop street, and he mashed down the brake. Next moment, Lee Lonnie had the door open and she jumped out and ran. As she ran, she kept screaming.

'Come back!' Rudd hollered after her, but the door slammed shut, cutting off his cry. And without his touching the foot feed, the Petey car scooted across the street, speeding up as it reached the other side. He trod down on the brake, and the brake didn't work for him. The Petey car ducked round a car just ahead and set sail for the edge of town.

'Help!' yelled Rudd, louder than Lee Lonnie had yelled. He grabbed for the emergency brake and couldn't find it. He tried to turn the wheel and go round a corner, and the wheel wouldn't turn. He went ransacking on in that runaway Petey car.

Better jump out, he told himself, jump out while you can. He was sailing along fast, but he had to risk it. He pushed down on the lever to open the door, and it wouldn't move. The glass was up three-quarters of the way, he couldn't dive out the window. He flung himself across to try to open the other door. He wasn't really surprised to find out that it wouldn't open either.

In his ears sounded a low, mournful note, maybe his blood racing or something about the car, he couldn't know which. Around another corner they went. He didn't even try to fight the wheel. He had never felt so helpless before. He wondered when they'd hit something and wished they would because that might stop them. But they didn't hit anything. They kept going in the night, with the headlights shining ahead on lawns and bushes. Now they were on Indian Rock Road. That's where old Mr Freddy had lived, there they went past his empty little house.

Passing it, the car turned off its light. They tore along Indian Rock Road in the night, under the branches of trees jamming across overhead, those trees that made noises and seemed to walk in the darkness. Rudd thought of getting into the back seat, trying one of the doors there. But he knew there'd be no sense to that. The Petey car stopped all of a sudden, so quickly he almost jammed against the steering wheel. The engine cut itself off, and there they stood in the silence.

He felt close and choked up in there, it was like being in a room full of wet old coats. He tried to rise, and something kept him down where he sat, something like a giant hand on his shoulder.

The voice he'd learned to know said, *Here we are* . . .

And there they were. Where? Why, right where old Mr Freddy Chunn had driven to die, when there wasn't anything else left for him to do. He'd driven there himself, but the Petey car had brought Rudd there. It knew what it was up to, it had known what it was up to every minute.

Heavy he felt, tons heavy with the weight on him, the air round him, hard to breathe, to brace his shoulders. Jen Bate had said something about being pressured, being pressed to death.

'I hadn't meant anything like killing!' he was barely able to whine out.

And the voice, speaking one more time: *But I do* . . .

He'd done everything wrong from the first. The way he'd nagged poor old Mr Freddy to death, the way he'd started driving the Petey car, the way he'd pestered Lee Lonnie. He knew that now. It weighed him down, like sacks and sacks of sand. He sank down against the wheel. His arms crossed themselves there. His head sank down on them. It came into his mind that he was sitting just the way Mr Freddy sat, when they found him dead.

But that's the last thought Rudd Stowe ever had on this earth.

Wood

by

ROBERT AICKMAN

Robert Aickman is the finest ghost story writer living; in this editor's opinion, he stands beside M. R. James as the finest of all time. He is the author of four collections of ghost stories: Dark Entries, Powers Of Darkness, Sub Rosa, Cold Hand In Mine, *and joint author of one more,* We Are For The Dark *(with Elizabeth Jane Howard). There are touches of the spectral in his first novel,* The Late Breakfasters, *and in* The Attempted Rescue, *the first volume of his autobiography. He has edited the eight* Fontana Books Of Great Ghost Stories, *some of which include perceptive and witty introductions. This is by no means all of his work, but it is warmly recommended to readers of this book.*

Some of his work – notably The Inner Room *– contains unnervingly adult echoes of fairy tales. 'Wood' does, but the story's haunting ambiguity is hardly for children, nor the easily disturbed.*

So my niece, Elinor, has given me one of those weather houses, where the woman comes out when it is likely to be fine, and the man when it is going to rain! I did not think they were made any more. There is something about them that not many people know; at least nowadays. It is this: that just as dowsing can be used to trace many things other than water (which of course makes 'water divining' quite the wrong name for it), so these little weather houses, or some of them, can be attuned to foretell more things than the merely literal state of the heavens.

It is an odd story of which I am reminded by this, and until now I have not cared to make a note of it. There is always a risk of a written record coming into the wrong hands; and so perhaps reaching the eyes or ears of the people described. Moreover, I was always very uncertain how far I could depend upon my own impressions of what happened; and naturally I am even less confident now, nearly twenty years later. Also, one is superstitious about seeming to give a new life, by writing about it, to something which has frightened one. The curious business about Munn and his wife, whatever I thought about the reality of it, even at the time, certainly frightened me – so much that I was the last person to be surprised by what happened to them in the end. But old Pell and his wife are dead now too. So here goes.

I suppose that if anyone at all reads what I am writing, it is more likely than not to be a stranger. A few sentences about myself had, therefore, better come first.

I served my articles as an architect, in the days when that was how one learned a profession, by working at practical and immediate problems from the first, instead of merely listening to lectures and doing exercises; and for several years I worked as an architectural assistant in a good office, doing well and having every prospect of starting in practice on my own. The tone was set in those days by architects such as Ernest George, and there seemed an unlimited number of costly country houses being built, pleasant work for all who had the social knack of getting it – which did not seem very difficult, as I look back on it. But then came the war, the first one, and the real one: the greatest mistake mankind ever made, in my opinion, but, curiously enough, one out of which I myself did quite well, at least in a sense. Before it was over, and to my considerable surprise, I found myself a lieutenant-colonel, though very much of the wartime kind, not the real thing, as I knew perfectly well; but then in the very last month, more or less when Wilfred Owen was killed, if I have it right, I was, not killed, but badly knocked out, since when I have never been quite right in any way, even though I made a good recovery, and a remarkably swift one.

Of course I had always intended to go back into architecture, but I never quite did. There were several factors. One was that I began to receive a pension, which at first seemed fairly good: enough, anyway, to save one from having to rush at things, and to give one time to think. Another, and much more important, was that the profession had completely changed. We were fast on the way to the state of affairs when the word 'art' was seldom mentioned, still less the word 'beauty'. It is odd that the busy, slave-driving old offices, always with several pupils, had much to say about art and beauty – too much, many of the pupils thought; while these new Schools of Architecture lead to nothing but, for example, the buildings you can see beside and around the Festival Hall in London. A third thing was that I never succeeded in marrying and thus taking on a new incentive. The war seemed to do something to me there; or perhaps it was mainly my experiences at the end of the war. But what settled things at first was that I was offered the job of editing a series of architectural lives.

I had always been interested in the actual lives and careers of the architects of history, and the work carried me away completely for a longish time. I was enabled to travel in a modest way (though, there again, I could not have paid for a wife to travel with me), and I was in a position to appoint myself as the author of two or three of the books. I did so, and these books proved to be among the most successful of the series, for what that meant. When I was in my mid-forties, I bought an old cottage outside this Suffolk village; without clearly realising that East Anglia is pre-eminently the part of England to which unattached and unattachable males with tiny, but comparatively secure incomes tend to drift. They settle there at the outskirts of villages, and, I must admit, seem often to live on for ever, though no one quite knows what they do all day. Edward Fitzgerald is the archetype and patron of us all; though, speaking for myself, I have so far managed to keep my hands off the local fishing lads. But then Fitzgerald was a genius, even though an under-productive one. I, no genius, have managed to have many affairs of the more ordinary kind; mainly, indeed, with married women. It does not seem a thing one should proclaim: but it is no joke being a married woman in East Anglia, if the woman has the smallest imagination. I am, therefore, unabashed.

That odd man, Munn, on the other hand, seemed, during the first years I knew him, to be genuinely uninterested in women. Of course I did not know him really well, then or ever; and one can be utterly mistaken in such assessments. Still, many English males *are* genuinely unconcerned about women; are without the need for them, especially after the age of thirty or so.

Munn struck me in those days as one who instead of embracing a woman, embraced a grievance. Unlike most people with entrenched grievances, he was as reticent about the details as one normally is, or as one should be, about the details of a love relationship. He had been employed in the Inland Revenue, and there had been trouble of some kind, though it was hard to guess what, because he had emerged with a small allowance, upon which, like me, he lived; in his case, in rooms above the village post office. Possibly he unearthed some corruption or other, and had to be sacked, and silenced. If Munn had been still in the employ of the tax people, instead of on bad terms with them, I could never have known him even as an acquaintance; because, say what they will, I cannot accept that any kind of gentleman will, under any circumstances, make a career of prying into the private affairs of others and then mulcting them, commonly to the point of spoiling and destroying their entire lives and those of their families. Munn supplemented his allowance (which, comically enough, was 'tax free') by making funny little figures out of straw and brass wire, which were offered for sale in the post office below under the name of 'daffies'. It was an unusual occupation for a middle-aged man, but I mention it because it had a faint and obscure bearing upon what happened in the future. Meanwhile, the figures, though often quite clumsy, seemed to sell remarkably well; not only to passing motorists, of whom, from other points of view, there were soon far too many, needless to say, but even to the villagers and to rustics apparently from other villages. Sometimes one of our locals, having bought one of Munn's straw figures, would later buy another. Perhaps the first figure had by then worn out, but at least it proved that Munn was meeting a demand, always the great thing in the world, we are told. I have described the figures as 'little', and so most of them were; but always on view were a few larger ones, two or three feet high. Naturally, these cost more, and it was the smaller, cheaper figures that most of the motorists went for, and that must have provided most of the turnover – again, as is usual in commerce.

Munn had taken up residence in the village before I arrived, and at first all I knew of him was his tweedy figure toddling about and sometimes bidding me good-day. His tweeds were very hairy indeed, and more than usually shapeless. One almost felt that he made his suits himself, as well as the straw figures; and perhaps wove the hirsute fabric also. He had profuse white hair under a scarecrow hat; a nose like a reversed peg for that same hat; and a dark red face, which made one think neither of drink nor of exposure to the elements, neither of sickness nor of shyness. It struck one simply as how he was made, how he was coloured; several shades too red, as some are made too tall, and others too dwarfish.

It was at one of the village inns (I refuse to employ the word 'pub') that I first exchanged more words with Munn than the time of day. I remember the occasion very well, but I have little recollection of what we said, then or, indeed, at most of our subsequent encounters. Of course he hinted at his troubles, and I at mine. But we were neither of us, perhaps to a fault, involved or much interested in what is called 'the life of the village', so that we undoubtedly ranged over wider fields: the newspapers, the world, and man's future (though, as I have said, seldom woman's). Munn seemed another who did not quite know what next to do in life, or even to aim at doing. He too was, more than anything else, marking time. The main thing we had in common was exile. All the remaining days of our lives seemed to drop upon us like dried-out snowflakes or like daily leaves from the dead calendar of a past and forgotten year. It was as well that the Marxists did not catch and roast us. Life has become more rigorous than it was then; though it is likely to become more rigorous still.

And yet –

I think I had been talking in a sketchy way to Munn, on and off, and every now and then, for as long as three or four years, when one morning, as I was on my way to something rather private, and was less than usually open to distraction, he hailed me from across the street and asked if I would look in at his place for a drink that same evening. I can see him as he did it, in my mind's eye, quite clearly: the white shutters across Gabb the butcher's window were behind him in the late autumn sunshine (so that it must presumably have been early closing day or the Sabbath). After all, it was a rather historic moment: I had never before been invited to enter the rooms above the post office. That which at the time I was about to undertake would be completed long before evening, so I accepted for half-past six.

Munn proved to have several rooms, quite a suite, reached by his own stair from the street; and, in general, seemed to be better accommodated than I had supposed, even though the trappings plainly appertained to a 'furnished apartment'. All that looked personal was a mill for making the straw figures. As usual with Munn, the device looked as if he had made it himself, out of rough old planks, long thick nails, and bright steel edges – very sharp, by the look of them. The contraption stood in a corner of the living room, with a bale of straw stuck away behind it, and straw ends all over the carpet beneath and around it. Of course, all was dry, or no doubt there would have been complaints from the sub-postmistress, Mrs Hextable, below. There were also two or three of the figures lying about in various stages of completion.

'My eker-out of income,' said Munn, entering the room behind me and watching my gaze. He crossed to the machine and gave it a hard kick in the midriff, so that the bright cutting wheel spun round like a flying saucer. 'And I wish His Majesty's bloody Commissioners were beneath it,' added Munn.

'But sit yourself down,' he went on, and, without consulting me, mixed a whisky that was far stronger than I normally liked or like, or than he had observed me drink at the inn, supposing that he ever took in such things. 'I propose to ask you a favour.'

He had provided himself with an even stronger whisky than mine. He gave me the impression of a man who so feared to find himself weak that he had both hands on the bull's horns almost before the animal had entered the field, so to speak.

'I'm getting married and I want you to be my best man.'

I must admit I had feared that it was going to be something to do with money.

'I expect I can manage that,' I replied, 'though it's something I've never done.'

'At our age, one feels such a fool at having to ask,' said Munn. I saw that his hands were shaking.

I have always felt that the plural possessive is a case that should be used with caution, but all I said was 'Where will it be? And who is she? And congratulations too, of course.'

'It's only in the next county. In fact, just over the border.' Munn expressed it a trifle histrionically, but of course there *is* an enormous difference between Suffolk and Norfolk, and between both and North Essex.

'I shall be hiring a motor,' Munn continued, staring at me, as if the availability of private transport might make all the difference.

'I shall be delighted to do everything I can,' I said, taking a goodish pull on Munn's whisky. 'In fact, I shall be honoured.'

Munn looked a shade doubtful about that, as well he might; but he was wonderfully relieved, and almost gulped as he said, 'Thank you very much. I shall never forget it. I may be able to do the same for you one day.'

'Who knows?' I responded, as the whisky began to rise within me.

'Would Saturday of the week after next suit you?' Munn really seemed to imply that if it would not, the day could be changed.

'Perfectly,' I replied; though almost completely at random.

'I was afraid it might not. Unfortunately it has to be on a Saturday or a Sunday, or my future wife's people couldn't get to it.'

'I quite understand.'

'He's a very busy man, and his wife is closely involved in what they do.'

It seemed that I was meant to take that up, even though, as will be noticed, I had not yet even learned the bride's name. 'And what is that?' I enquired politely.

'It's something I think you ought to know. That's why I raised the matter,' said Munn.

I nodded.

'It's a little hard to talk about,' said Munn, looking at the floor. 'It's the kind of thing that makes people giggle a bit.' Munn drew on himself again and gazed at me. 'I don't really mind if you do giggle. I couldn't possibly blame you.'

'I shall do nothing of the kind,' I rejoined.

But Munn still beat about the bush. 'You know that story of Maurice Baring's? Or is it a play?'

'I am not sure that I do.' Maurice Baring had, after all,

written an enormous amount even by the date we had then reached.

'A young man tells a girl he has a secret that he simply must confide in her before she marries him. She swears black and blue that no matter what it may be, she will love him as much as ever. In the end, he discloses that he's the hangman, and she sheers off.'

'No,' I said. 'I can't recall having come upon that.'

'My future father-in-law is an undertaker,' said Munn. 'Not the hangman. Just the undertaker.'

'I shouldn't let that worry you. Indeed, I've always understood it's a most lucrative trade. Whatever happens in the world, the demand's still there. Indeed, as things get worse, it often increases.'

'What a good chap you are!' exclaimed Munn, refilling my glass. 'When I told my brother, he laughed at first, and then began to be very wary. Of course he's been a married man for more than twenty years. Really settled, is Rodney. But it was just the same with three other men I spoke to about it.'

'It doesn't worry me,' I asserted. It was hardly possible to say anything else, though what I had said was not the exact truth.

'It's just the two of them do the whole thing,' Munn continued. 'He was a merchant-navy carpenter or something like that to begin with, and then began to specialise. She does the laying-out, as I believe it's still called. I'm told she can do the other things too; as well as any professional. Embalming, for example; though of course there's no great demand for that in rural England. All the same, she has an embalmer's full certificate. It's rather comic really. It hangs on their wall. It's one of the first things you see.'

'Someone has to do these things,' I said.

'Yes,' said Munn. 'And it's quite surprising how clean and calm it all is when you get close to it. "Clean" and "calm" are the words that have stayed in my mind all the way through.'

I enquired no further, though I daresay it was obvious enough that Munn wanted to go on talking around the discouraging topic. For my part, I have always been a conventional enough person, and, drink or no drink, I was beginning very clearly to understand why the topic is half-taboo. I said I was sorry but that it was time I went, and Munn said he would call for me in the hired motor at eight a.m. on the following Saturday week. Did I mind it being so early? Munn was once more drawing himself together. But I was past minding almost anything, as long as this absurd ceremony could be decently put into the past, and, as far as I was concerned, buried there. I said I would look for a booklet upon the duties of a best man, but Munn said quite earnestly that it wouldn't be necessary.

In all the circumstances, I never expected to receive one of those smooth cards that announce future weddings; and this was as well, because none came. Before the day dawned, I saw Munn, two or three times, stumbling about the village. After all, it was not a large village, and an imminent bridegroom could hardly live as a recluse. I thought it best to make no approach, and this was clearly right, because Munn made no approach to me, except that once when we were far enough apart and unmistakably going in different directions, he winked at me. It seemed plain that Munn did not want his future plans to be generally discussed, so I said nothing about the matter to anyone. After a day or two, however, I recollected that a best man is expected to make a presentation of some kind to the bride. The answer to that was simpler than might be expected: I have a rule that when a gift is required, I give a year's membership (or, occasionally, longer) of a society which admits one free of charge to a number of buildings of diverse architectural interest. The general public has to pay for admission in every case; and the list of structures includes several important ones to which the general public is not admitted at all. I did reflect that it might not be an absolutely ideal gift for a young girl, but there was no evidence that Munn's intended *was* a young girl. I knew nothing about her. I had not enquired, because I had little doubt that if Munn had wanted me to know at that stage, he would have told me. There was also the question of gifts to the bridesmaids. I dealt with it by assuming that there would be no bridesmaids.

I was right about that, but, for some reason (no doubt, the infrequency of weddings in my life), it had never occurred to me that there might not even be a church.

'I simply couldn't face all that white stuff and slobbering about,' said Munn to me in the car. 'I'm sure you'll agree it's not the thing for chaps of our age.'

So we were making towards a small country town with a convenient registry office. I shall not give a name to the town, because marriage is an institution so delicate that all in any way concerned are very touchy on the subject, and prone to seek legal redress for any possible dubiety or even comment. At the time, I wondered whether Munn was not perhaps a divorced man; or even a potential bigamist. It was the kind of thing that the course of events tended to bring to one's mind; but I have absolutely no reason to think there was any truth in either hypothesis.

In the car, however, Munn did let fall his bride's family name. It was Pell: in East Anglia, a gypsy name, though less eminent in that way than Mace. I did not remark upon these facts to Munn. He was now referring to the bride herself as 'Vi'. Munn struck me as being less uneasy than I had expected. I observed that he had not bought new clothes for the occasion, but was in his usual shapeless tweeds. I myself was at least wearing a 'dark suit'. I touched my pocket containing the membership card of the society I have mentioned, which I had sealed in an envelope: sealed, I mean, with scarlet sealing wax. I was far from sure what would be the best moment to hand it over. I should have to wait upon events.

The distance was not all that great and we managed to arrive before the registry office was even open. There were, in fact, six or seven minutes to go. I felt that this was the sort of thing that could be counted upon, and concentrated upon the idea that my duties must soon be all over. At least we had the car to wait in; which was fortunate, as it had begun to rain. The car was of moderate size only, and I wondered how many there would be for the return trip. The young driver began to nod to passers-by he knew. Munn had fallen silent. By way of conversation, I enquired how he and his bride had met.

'She came into the post office and liked my straw daffies. She told Mrs Hextable that she would like to meet me. She thought we had interests in common. Mrs Hextable came up and brought me down. And so it proved to be.'

'You mean that you *did* find you had a lot in common?'

'So it seemed. I must admit that I'd been keeping half an eye open for a wife for some time. You may not believe that. I was feeling more and more that I couldn't let my whole life be ruined by the swinish way I was treated.'

'Of course I believe you, and I'm quite sure you're right,' I said firmly; 'and I very sincerely hope you'll be very happy.' I felt quite warm about it.

'Old Pell says he's going to build us a house,' remarked Munn.

I managed to avoid any facetious reference to an abode which would last till Doomsday. Even so, Munn was blushing slightly.

'My God!' I cried. 'What about the ring?' It was the first I had thought of it. I was behaving like the best man in a pantomime, but then, of course, one so often does behave like a character in a pantomime.

'It's all right,' said Munn. 'Here it is.' He handed over a tiny grey box from his jacket pocket.

'Isn't it rather small?'

'She's a small girl.'

At that point, one of the big office doors opened and a clerk emerged.

'Is either of you Mr Munn?'

'I am,' said Munn.

'The Registrar's waiting for you. The bride is inside already with her family.' I cannot recall that I ever learned how they had managed to achieve this: professional influence, no doubt.

We followed the clerk indoors, and, slightly to my surprise, the young driver of the car came after us. As Munn made no objection, it was not for me to speak.

The windows of the room in which the ceremony was to take place were in need of cleaning. Perhaps they were unusually difficult to reach, as they were very high in the walls. The grime on the panes and the increasing rainfall made things very dim, and somewhat obscured my first view of the Pell family.

My main feeling was that they were indeed small: small, smooth, and round was the impression they all left with me. Miss Pell, a little taller than her gnome-like parents, though only a trifle, was a pretty, round-faced, round-eyed girl, arrayed in bright colours, a selection of them. She had very blue eyes and very pink cheeks and very yellow hair, which stuck up sturdily all over her head, rather in the manner of Munn's own white tangle. She was talking as we entered the room, in a noticeably sharp, even metallic voice; there was something stocky and assured in her whole demeanour, which, I must admit, did not attract me; and from pretty well the first instant I was in no doubt at all that it was she who had carried off Munn rather than he who had captured her. Why she should wish to do that was another matter; but no affair of mine, and rather glad I was to be so unimplicated. Munn's marriage, hitherto partly comic, partly pathetic, became for me, as I entered that registry office, partly disagreeable as well . . . I should add that little Mr Pell was dressed in a well-fitted black suit, and little Mrs Pell in a tight dress of deepest purple.

'Happy to meet you,' said Mr Pell. One simply could not exclude the sinister overtones of such a greeting from one's mind, absurd though it is to say so.

I simpered.

'I often think the best man is the key to the whole wedding,' continued Mr Pell. Even that implausible compliment added to my uneasiness, lacking as I was in all experience of the tasks required. Moreover, Mr Pell had a grating voice; compulsive antecedent of his daughter's.

'How do you like the bride's clothes?' enquired Mrs Pell. 'Doesn't she look gay? Don't you think Leonard's lucky to get her?' I had forgotten that Munn's name was Leonard (Christian names were not used among men in the present casual way), and had to grope in my mind for what she meant.

'She looks lovely,' I said.

'You'll be able to kiss her in a few minutes, you know. It's the best man's privilege.'

'I shan't forget.'

But the Registrar was awaiting us with some impatience, especially as he had a bad cold. The rubric was minimal, so that only a few minutes had seemingly passed before he was saying 'And I hope you'll be very happy,' and moving back to the fire that was smoking away in his private room. I had passed across the ring at the right moment and, at so spare a solemnisation, had little other commitment. We all signed the register, including the driver of the car. There had been no one else present, except the registrar's clerk, who served unobtrusively.

The Pells were cackling away (the verb is unavoidable: though of course voices do run in families, as do handwritings and faiths), and now had come the time for me to kiss Vi. Her cheek (to which I confined myself) struck me as hard and chilly, but the bride is in a palpably false position at such moments. All the same, I remembered by contrast other kisses that were coming my way just then. I also noticed that Munn

had not kissed Vi at all. He had not touched her in any way
except to put the small ring on her stick-like finger. The rain
had eased off when we emerged, so I suppose it may all have
taken rather longer than I supposed.

To my relief, there was no further celebration. Even drinks
all round at the hotel opposite were precluded by the licensing
hours, as we all had to agree. Munn, the new Mrs Munn, and
I re-entered the car and the Pells waved us away. I saw their
squat shapes shoulder to shoulder on the pavement: Mr Pell
with his right arm raised, Mrs Pell with her left. The rain was
now only a light drizzle, to which the Pells seemed imper-
vious. After all, most funerals take place in the wet, I reflected.
Could it have been really so difficult for Pell to get away thus
briefly and thus early on another day than Saturday? Not that
it mattered. I remembered that the Pells had had to travel from
somewhere or other. I do not think I then knew where Pell
plied his profession: visibly, as I had seen for myself, happier
than any lark, as are all these men of timber and satin.

Munn was taking his bride back to the rooms over the post
office. I had found them, of course, to be more spacious than I
had thought before I entered them. I noticed that the word
'honeymoon' was never, in my hearing, mentioned. In the
car, however, Vi, from the back seat, did assure me anxiously
that, as Munn had said, her father was going to build them a
house.

'The first thing we'll do,' she grated on, 'is start looking for
a plot. It'll have to be the cheapest we can find, as Daddy
doesn't believe in buying things when he can make so much
with his own hands.'

There was no reference to Munn making any contribution,
nor did he, installed in the back seat beside her, say a word.

'It will only be a teeny house,' Vi explained in her rasping
voice, 'but Mummy says you're often best off when you're
living small.'

It was necessary to enter into it. 'Have you a builder in
mind?' I enquired.

'Of course not, silly. Daddy's going to build it for us.'

I had sensed that this was in the background. 'The whole thing?' I asked. 'The plumbing included? And the electricity?' The latter had just entered our area, but was not yet truthfully in our immediate range.

'We shan't be having silly things like that. Only wood.'

I was constrained to turn in my seat, difficult though it was to do, and look back at her.

'Daddy can make everything needed in this world out of wood.'

There was something almost evangelical in her tone and choice of words. There was also something wild and fantastical: which seemed infectious.

'Even people?' I asked, smiling no doubt, but really asking under some compulsion that remained elusive.

'You're making game of me,' she replied on the instant. Her pink cheeks had darkened, and I noticed that she, for her part, was not smiling at all.

'Lay off, you fool,' said Munn, really quite sharply, and speaking almost for the first time since entering the car. 'Let's change the subject. We haven't even started looking for the land as yet.'

'That's right,' said Vi. 'Though we're going to, aren't we, Leonard?' She left little doubt that they were.

And we did manage to talk of something else. As a matter of fact, we talked of how beautiful the wedding had been: a compulsory theme, needless to say, for all such moments of time, regardless of objectivity.

Munn had been preposterously rude; but I had observed such quick gripings of rage in him before, notably when he thought about the Inland Revenue and how they had treated him.

A few weeks later, the Munns did invite me round one evening, 'after supper'. It was a remarkably formal visit: I must acknowledge that I found it difficult to keep the word 'wooden' out of my mind. Munn's capacity to talk at large about this and that, seemed entirely to have shrivelled, as happens so often to a man after marriage, sometimes immediately after; and Vi's sole interest appeared to be her own family and their conversationally equivocal trade.

Inevitably no doubt, she took the line that there was nothing whatever to be frightened about, and that the details were most interesting when encountered from the inside. The expression 'from the inside' did not appeal to me. And, with Vi, it was difficult even to make a feeble joke about it; or, I thought, about anything.

I learned that the constructions in which her father took so much pride, and she on his behalf, were passed off, at least within the family firm, as 'boxes'. It was not that this usage was specially defined to me. It was simply that the words 'box' and 'boxes', with various other special expressions were lightly thrown about by Vi, and sometimes by Munn too; so that I quickly realised what was meant, as when one grasps a foreign idiom through contact with those to whom it is habitual.

Thus Vi remarked: 'Daddy's already made our boxes'; as one might lightly describe the planting of two saplings by way of commemoration.

It was impossible not to perceive that Munn seemed already to be completely involved; to be seriously and sincerely interested in the gruesome business. Again it is something one commonly notes: that very speedily the husband is all but totally englutinated into the wife's life pattern.

Perhaps in the present case, a kind of clue was offered – or reoffered.

'As soon as I set eyes on those daffies Leonard made,' observed Vi, her round blue eyes almost alive, 'I *knew*.'

And, this time, suddenly, I knew too. Munn's reference to something of the same kind, when he was asking me to be his best man, had left me groping after some mere folksiness, some rural witchery and magic, which one could only hope was white. Now I realised that, at least for Vi, Munn's journeyman imitations of men (if I may cite Hamlet) were surrogates for those other imitations of men that were put into her father's boxes. (For what, at the end, is man but ravelled straw?)

Munn's cups and plates or Mrs Hextable's, had all disappeared, and we ate little square sandwiches, with pink stuff inside, off smooth wooden platters, and drank tea out of mugs that had been not thrown but hollowed out. In the end, when Vi was out of the room, Munn offered me a whisky, and whipped out a single glass tumbler from the back of the cupboard.

He drank nothing himself, though before he had customarily exceeded me.

'I've been looking around,' he said, in a confidential voice. 'The daffies won't keep two of us, nor will my measly blood money.' It struck me that it was the first time that evening he had referred, even indirectly, to the King Charles's Head which previously had floated almost all the time before his angry gaze. 'And soon there'll be three of us.'

'Indeed?' I replied. I reflected, in a vulgar way, that it seemed quick work. 'I congratulate you both.'

'Vi sets great store by our having a child immediately. And so do her people.'

'I see what you mean,' I said. 'And have you found anything?'

'No, damn it, I haven't. It's not easy at our age. But I have something in the back of my mind.'

'And what is that? If you wish to tell me, of course.'

'Not just yet, old man.' I could hear Vi approaching from the next room. 'Only if it materialises.'

The door opened. 'If what materialises, Leonard?' enquired Vi, in her unpleasant voice, her head on one side, like the head of a toy bird.

'If Marley's ghost materialises,' said Munn; with more authority than I had observed in him during the whole of the earlier evening.

Vi projected her straight red tongue at him from her round red mouth.

'All things come to him who waits,' said Munn with apparent vagueness. Married couples quickly learn to fill in with such utterances.

But I never really like drinking alone, so I soon made my excuses, and walked home to my cottage at the outskirts of the community.

I had a strong suspicion of what the something was at the back of Munn's mind.

And soon we walked into one another outside one of the branch banks. Not that either of us ran an account there: if one knows one's onions, one does not bank in one's own gossipy village.

'We're off,' Munn said. 'Vi and I. Next week, in fact: Wednesday, I'm told. The old man's sending one of his waggons. It's the only day he can spare one.'

'Waggons' in the patois of the Pell family had an implication similar to that of 'boxes'; so that the symbolism behind Munn's remarks seemed greatly too oppressive.

But Munn continued the theme. 'I doubt whether we shall meet again, you and I.'

For a moment I could find nothing at all to say, even though words were my trade.

Munn eased matters. 'Not that I shan't send you a change of address,' he said. 'Of course, I shall.'

'In that case,' I observed, smiling, 'I am sure we shall meet. I shall make a point of looking you up.'

'Don't speak too soon. You don't know what I shall be doing.'

'I think I do know.'

'I'm going into the old man's trade.'

'Yes?'

'I'm to serve a quick apprenticeship, to learn from the bottom up, so to speak. And, after that, there's a partnership offered ... So you'll hardly want to know me any more.'

'Nonsense,' I responded, as brightly as I could manage. 'Not see that charming girl you've discovered for yourself! Miss seeing your child! Not likely.' To so many married men, one has to say such things. One feels it is the least one can do; and that it is expected.

'You're a good chap,' said Munn, 'but, for God's sake, don't feel in the least obliged. I know what I'm doing and what the consequences are.'

'All bosh,' I rejoined, in the same spirit as before. 'You're taking up one of the safest money-spinners there is, and I look to enjoy some pickings from the rich man's table.'

I received a card bearing Munn's new address (it also bore a faint fringe of acorns), from which for the first time I learned the name of the settlement where the Pells did their work; and, as it happened, I also saw Pell's 'waggon', an outsize model, looking all the blacker for its bulk, as it bore away such of the trappings as were Munn's, and Munn himself on the seat in front, with the sable-accoutred driver at the other end, and little Vi wedged between them. It was evening at the time, and rapidly sinking into dusk. I reflected that public use of a 'waggon' for such an uncanonical purpose as this might attract adverse comment if done during the hours of full daylight. As for me, at that moment, I too had a particular reason for sliding about inconspicuously. Indeed, I drew far back into a convenient hedge as the huge 'waggon' sped smoothly by.

I did not go after the 'waggon' that week, or the following week; that month, or the following month; that year, or the following year. The place where the Pells had proved to live was a small industrial town, built, in remote East Anglia, as a single entity during the nineteenth century. Though high ideals lay behind its founding, it had little current reputation for beauty of architecture. Of course, standards change remarkably in such contexts, but, at the time I am talking about, the town was represented as a place more to avoid than to visit. Nor did I receive a specific invitation from the Munns. I had not expected one. Indeed, I received no further communication at all from them; not even an undertaker's Christmas card.

Some years later, none the less, I drifted over, and so acquired some idea of what ultimately became of Munn.

By then I had acquired a small, second-hand motor; a two-seater so-called roadster. For some time, I had had a commission to catalogue all the churches in Suffolk. It was no light or brief task, as Suffolk has many churches. Moreover, the prospect of a similar assignment relating to Norfolk was held before me. As far as pleasure went, I should greatly have preferred to travel by train and on foot, which was then perfectly possible; but my employers pressed. I am not sure that by the end, time had been saved; because my second-hand roadster was always breaking down and leaving me helpless, as I have no gift with machines and no love for them.

I acknowledge that for some time I omitted consideration of the town which housed the Pells (and which I had taken to thinking of always in that way). After all, it was agreed that the place had little to offer the connoisseur of beaux arts; such as was expected to study my careful lists. I was even ignoring the district around it; which, indeed, was still, in the main, open heath, with few churches, and hardly more houses. (Now it has been utilised in familiar ways: varying from an 'open prison' to a large mineral development.) But, in the end, necessity called, and, picking a rainy day, I set out. I should have preferred to disguise myself.

In the town itself, all went perfectly well, even though the rain inconveniently ceased to fall while I was doing my duty in the church. I recalled that the same had happened during Munn's inauspicious nuptials. The church, paid for entirely from the pocket of the founding industrialist, was splendidly ornate; after the fashion then, in the 1920's, deprecated, but now once more respected. The town, as a whole, duly seemed more of sociological than aesthetic interest. But my obligation was exclusively ecclesiastical; and though, as I edged along the streets, I kept half an eye open for the name PELL surmounted by plumes or the staring eyes of black horses, I saw nothing of the kind, and in the end even plucked up courage for a coffee and cake in an anomalous teashop, half gentlewoman's chintz and half charge hand's lincrusta. In those days, it was easier to 'park' one's car; though, on the other hand, one's car could therefore stand out more conspicuously.

It was on a low ridge to the south of the town, as I drove homewards, that I came upon Munn's new home. Curiously enough, I was deliberately avoiding any kind of main route, and weaving my way through lanes by the use of the map. This was not easy to combine with driving the roadster, but fortunately the lanes carried very little traffic in those days. Possibly there was some finger of fate which pointed my way to the house. I seemed conscious all along of such an element in my relationship with Munn; and what happened next perhaps confirms it.

It was hard to believe that it had been necessary to pay money for the 'plot' on which the house stood. The tiny, black structure recalled what one had heard of 'squatters' and their 'rights'. It stood on a sandy, scrubby, nondescript waste, like a thrown-away cabin trunk; or perhaps like a house built by the little people, there one day, gone the next. I am sure I should have known at once that it was the house built by Munn's father-in-law for his chicks with his own hands; but, as it happened, Vi, in her bright colours, was at work in the front garden as my open roadster snorted laboriously up the ridge. At the same time, rain began to fall once more, this time heavily. I saw Vi go back into the little house; from the other side of which Munn emerged, already clad in heavy oilskins. I suppose it was natural enough for the frail female to withdraw from the inclement weather and for the stouter male to take her place; but there seemed to me something odd and automatic about it, all the same. Moreover, on the instant two flaps opened in the house's single black gable, and a quite life-size wooden cuckoo jumped out, shouting its head off four times. I looked at my watch: it was indeed four o'clock. It seemed odd to have a clock outside a tiny private house, as if it were a town hall; but there could be no doubt about the hour of day being audible over a wide area.

By this time, Munn had looked up and seen me seated there, grinding slowly uphill. To speak plainly, I doubt whether, if I had been travelling faster, I should have stopped; though this may make me sound a cad. With Munn's gaze upon me, I had no alternative. Also, I should have to raise the hood; always a lengthy and injurious undertaking.

I brought the motor to a standstill. Munn just stood there staring at me, silent and motionless. His clothes had never appeared particularly to fit, as I believe I have indicated; but the oilskins seemed to belong to another and much larger man altogether. Munn held a hoe with a very long handle; but it was hard to see what he was doing with it, or what Vi had been doing before him. I have spoken of 'a front garden', but when I stopped the car, I realised that there was nothing: no cultivation of any kind, but only the sparse and stony heath, no different in front of the house from elsewhere.

'Excuse me,' I shouted, 'I must put up my hood.' By now the rain was bucketing down; what people call a 'cloudburst', though no one knows exactly what that is. Raising the hood was always a fearful ploy, but I dashed at it and did better than usual under the continued pressures of the situation. All the same, the job took a minute or two, so that it became rather noticeable that Munn was not offering to help.

When I had adjusted the last screw (car hoods were more elaborately devised in early days), I realised that Munn was no longer there at all. Obviously, instead of coming to my aid, he had returned to the house for shelter.

I think I should almost certainly have proceeded therewith upon my way, though no doubt with qualms. But what happened was that the car refused to start; which was all too customary.

I sat there for some time with the downpour beating on the hood. I daresay I fiddled around a little with the levers and buttons and so forth, but I had little hope in that direction.

Then I noticed that the glass in the front windows of Munn's house was broken. They were narrow French windows; narrow, but a pair of them. And it was not just a matter of the glass being cracked, but of actual black holes. From the whole look of the place, it dawned on me that no one could seriously live there. And yet, without doubt, I had seen both Munn and Mrs Munn. The former had stared, quite unmistakably, at me, for an appreciable period of time.

Hitherto I had spent the day (and long before that) beating around the bush in one way and another precisely in order not to re-encounter these Munns and Pells. It now occurred to me that the tribe of them had perhaps so weighed upon my mind that I was seeing members of it where they were not. The little black house was so exactly what I was both looking for and avoiding, that the notion of an hallucination seemed slightly more plausible than it commonly does. I had even heard or read that hallucinations are most likely at just such moments between dark and light as, with the heavily gathering clouds, I had lately passed through.

Perhaps for reasons such as these, perhaps for obscurer, and less resistible reasons, at which I have hinted, I resolved to have a closer look round. I was wearing a motorist's overcoat, substantial even against such weather as this. I climbed down from the car and walked over to the broken windows. There was no hedge, gate, or boundary of any kind.

I looked in, with some caution, through one of the holes in

the glass; while the rain from the wide gable above dripped down my neck. Despite the two French doors, there appeared to be only a single room within, stretching from side to side of the house; and with the inside walls painted in the same black as the outside. There were some vague items of litter lying about the floor, but no real furniture that I could see. All the same, I could hear the huge cuckoo cloak ticking above my head; and someone, I reflected, had to wind it ... Or perhaps not. Perhaps Mr Pell could make entirely wooden clocks that required no winding.

I was not yet exactly frightened, but, rather, puzzled. I pushed away at both the French windows, but succeeded only in dislodging further portions of glass, which fell to the black floor inside with astonishingly much noise. I half expected the life-size cuckoo upstairs to croak in protest.

I imagined that there might be a door at the back of the structure; through which, as I could not help thinking, one 'got at the works', in little houses and like artefacts made of wood. I walked round in the rain, and such a door there was. This time, I dragged it open. It stuck and shrieked, but by now I meant business and I pulled hard.

The first thing I saw inside was a child seated on a shelf with both arms extended. It was presumably clutching something out of sight at each side; as its whole posture suggested strain and effort. At first, I thought, however absurdly, that it was a real child; but I realised that it was a figure in wood of remarkable liveliness. I even managed to extend my hand and touch it. It felt like wood too.

The little house was divided into two chambers by a wooden partition which, painted in the usual black, now confronted me, and against which the child's shelf was set on wooden brackets. This rear chamber was six or eight feet deep. The door I had opened was a large one and admitted a considerable amount of light, except into the further corners; but there was no window, and the carefully painted, elaborately life-like figure of the child had been sitting there, it was impossible to guess for how long, in complete darkness. All things considered, it was surprisingly well preserved and spruce.

I now saw that its two hands were involved with a system of wires and pulleys which went upwards into the dimness, but was rusty, broken, and drooping. Here were indeed the customary 'works'. I thought it might be an unusually complex scheme for manipulating the marionette that squatted before me; but it then seemed to me more as though it were the child, with its cogent posture, that was designed to do the manipulation. And the child was so shiny and glossy, where all else was so rotten. *Quis custodiet ipsos custodes?* I could not help asking myself.

Beneath the shelf was a low door into the main room of the house, this time ajar. I kicked it open, bent myself double (which was not easy in my very heavy coat), and went through.

The litter on the floor, not merely dusty and dirty, but damp and fungoid, proved to be mainly pages from a book or booklet on the collection of taxes. Against the back partition wall, to the right of the door as I looked back at it, was what appeared, after all, to be the ruin of a large, low piece of furniture. It was as dark, as black, as everything else, and I had not made it out when I peered in through the French windows at the front.

I saw that to the inside of the dwarf-sized door a piece of paper had been pasted: the instructions, one could not help thinking, upon how to get the best out of the device. I went back and peered. Instructions, after a kind, indeed they were; written out in ink and with no punctuation by a hand to me unknown. I read them; and after a considerable pause brought out my churches notebook from my jacket pocket, and copied them down. Here is what I wrote:

> *When the man is sawing wood*
> *Wait and watch for falling blood*

> *Blood and sawdust are the same*
> *In Dame Nature's little game.*
>
> *When the woman's blindly scraping*
> *Then's the hour for blows and raping*
> *Within the earth without a sound*
> *That's what makes the world go round.*
>
> *Whatever else you need to know*
> *Set the man and woman so*
> *Let them prophesy for ever*
> *Curse them once and come back never.*

Obediently, I gazed around me. I thought that, before departing, I might as well look more closely at the low piece of crumbling furniture set against the partition wall.

There could be no doubt as to what was really there. The 'piece of crumbling furniture' was a pair of old Mr Pell's 'boxes'; set side by side and crumbling indeed. They had no lids – perhaps the lids had crumbled quite away; and inside were the remains, respectively, of the late Mr and Mrs Munn, in no ordinary state of decomposition, but half-merged, in fact much more than half, into the wood from which and to which I was beginning to think we all spring and return. Like a pair of Daphnes, the two of them I thought; Daphne who was changed by Apollo into a tree. Not that the hideous amalgam in those boxes was imperishable. Far from that; it was already turning into a woody, crawling, wretchedness, damp and primeval-looking, flesh and pulp as one... Daphne? Of what, in that wooden house, did the name remind me? Then of course I remembered. Old Munn's 'daffies' ... I could only wonder.

I made a bolt for it, not looking back, least of all at the little fellow on the shelf, but slamming the door as I ran, so that it jammed fast.

Believe it or not, I had quite forgotten that my car was

broken down. I gave one twirl on the starter, leapt in, and had roared on for at least a mile and a half before I recollected that by rights I should not be moving – or escaping – at all. The finger of fate once more, I could not but feel.

And perhaps the spell was, in fact, now broken; because, only a few weeks later, I read in the local weekly that there had been a bad fire one night on the heath, with many sheds and shanties burnt out, and several lives lost. In the way of local weeklies, the report concluded by saying that the funerals of the victims would be conducted by Mr Pell.

The Pattern

by

RAMSEY CAMPBELL

Ramsey Campbell (1946–) won't refer to himself in the third person; it sounds schizophrenic. My first published story appeared in 1962, from Arkham House; I'm another of the writers Arkham helped. Since 1973 I've been a full-time writer. I also lecture, review films for Radio Merseyside, comics for the British Fantasy Society.

Lovecraft and M. R. James influenced my fiction; so did the guidance of August Derleth. My work has appeared in many anthologies and magazines. My books include The Inhabitant Of The Lake, Demons By Daylight, The Height Of The Scream, *and a horror novel,* The Doll Who Ate His Mother, *soon to be published by Star.*

Some informed friends read the first tale I wrote for this book. They were dissatisfied with it, and rightly: my thanks to Ted Klein, Kathy Murray, and Hugh Lamb. Later I wrote the following, and believe I'm right to use it here.

Di seemed glad when he went outside. She was sitting on the settee, legs shoved beneath her, eyes squeezed tight, looking for the end of her novel. She acknowledged the sound of the door with a short nod, pinching her mouth as if he'd been distracting her. He controlled his resentment; he'd often felt the same way about her, while painting.

He stood outside the cottage, gazing at the spread of green.

Scattered buttercups crystallised the yellow tinge of the grass. At the centre of the field a darker green rushed up a thick tree, branching, multiplying; towards the edges of the field, bushes were foaming explosions, blue-green, red-edged green. Distant trees displayed an almost transparent papery spray of green. Beyond them lay curves of hills, toothed with tiny pines and a couple of random towers, all silver as mist. As Tony gazed, sunlight spilled from behind clouds to the sound of a huge soft wind in the trees. The light filled the greens, intensifying them; they blazed.

Yes, he'd be able to paint here. For a while he had feared he wouldn't. He'd imagined Di struggling to find her final chapter, himself straining to paint, the two of them chafing against each other in the little cottage. But good Lord, this was only their second day here. They weren't giving themselves time. He began to pace, looking for the vantage-point of his painting.

There were patterns and harmonies everywhere. You only had to find them, find the angle from which they were clear to you. He had seen that one day, while painting the microcosm of patterns in a patch of verdure. Now he painted nothing but glimpses of harmony, those moments when distant echoes of colour or movement made sense of a whole landscape; he painted only the harmonies, abstracted. Often he felt they were glimpses of a total pattern that included him, Di, his painting, her writing, life, the world: his being there and seeing was part of the pattern. Though it was impossible to perceive the total pattern, the sense was there. Perhaps that sense was the purpose of all real art.

Suddenly he halted. A May wind was passing through the landscape. It unfurled through the tree in the field; in a few moments the trees beyond the field responded. It rippled through the grass, and the lazy grounded swaying echoed the leisurely unfolding of the clouds. All at once he saw how the clouds elaborated the shapes of the trees and bushes, subtracting colour, lazily changing their shapes as they drifted across the sky.

He had it now. The wind passed, but it didn't matter. He could paint what he'd seen; he would see it again when the breeze returned. He was already mixing colours in his mind, feeling enjoyment begin: nobody could ever mass-produce the colours he saw. He turned towards the cottage, to tiptoe upstairs for his canvas and the rest without disturbing Di.

Behind him someone screamed.

In the distance, across the field. One scream: the hills echoed curtly. Tony had to grab an upright of the cottage porch to steady himself. Everything snapped sharp, the cottage garden, the uneven stone wall, the overgrown path beyond the wall, the fence and the wide empty flower-sprinkled field. There was nobody in sight. The echoes of the cry had stopped at once, except in Tony's head. The violence of the cry reverberated there. Of what emotion? Terror, outrage, disbelief, agony? All of them?

The door slammed open behind him. Di emerged, blinking red-eyed, like an angrily roused sleeper. 'What's wrong?' she demanded nervously. 'Was that you?'

'I don't know what it was. Over there somewhere.'

He was determined to be calm. The cry had unnerved him; he didn't want her nervousness to reach him too – he ignored it. 'It might have been someone with their foot in a trap,' he said. 'I'll see if I can see.'

He backed the car off the end of the path, onto the road. Di watched him over the stone wall, rather anxiously. He didn't really expect to find the source of the cry; probably its cause was past now. He was driving away from Di's edginess, to give her a chance to calm down. He couldn't paint while he was aware of her nervousness.

He drove. Beside the road the field stretched placidly, easing the scream from his mind. Perhaps someone had just stumbled, had cried out with the shock. The landscape looked too peaceful for anything worse. But for a while he tried to remember the sound, some odd quality about it that nagged at him. It hadn't sounded quite like a cry; it had sounded as if – It was gone.

He drove past the far side of the field beyond the cottage. A path ran through the trees along the border; Ploughman's Path, a sign said. He parked and ventured up the path a few hundred yards. Patches of light flowed over the undergrowth, blurring and floating together, parting and dimming. The trees were full of the intricate trills and chirrups of birds. Tony called out a few times: 'Anyone there? Anybody hurt?' But the leaves hushed him.

He drove further uphill, towards the main road. He would return widely around the cottage, so that Di could be alone for a while. Sunlight and shadow glided softly over the Cotswold hills. Trees spread above the road, their trunks lagged with ivy. Distant foliage was a bank of green folds, elaborate as coral.

On the main road he found a pub, the Farmer's Rest. That would be good in the evenings. The London agent hadn't mentioned that; he'd said only that the cottage was isolated, peaceful. He'd shown them photographs, and though Tony had thought the man had never been near the cottage, Di had loved it at once. Perhaps it was what her book needed.

He glimpsed the cottage through a gap in the hills. Its mellow Cotswold stone seemed concentrated, a small warm amber block beyond the tiny tree-pinned field, a mile below. The green of the field looked simple now, among the fields where sheep and cattle strolled sporadically. He was sorry he'd come so far from it. He drove towards the turn-off that would take him behind the cottage and eventually back to its road.

Di ran to the garden wall as he drove onto the path. 'Where were you?' she said. 'I was worried.'

Oh Christ, he thought, defeated. 'Just looking. I didn't find anything. Well, I found a pub on the main road.'

She tutted at him, smiling wryly: just like him, she meant. 'Are you going to paint?'

She couldn't have made any progress on her book; she would find it even more difficult now. 'I don't think so,' he said.

'Can't you work either? Oh, let's forget it for today. Let's walk to the pub and get absolutely pissed.'

At least the return journey would be downhill, he thought, walking. A soft wind tugged at them whenever they passed gaps; green light and shadow swarmed among branches. The local beer was good, he found. Even Di liked it, though she wasn't fond of beer. Among the Toby jugs and bracketed rifles, farmers discussed dwindling profits, the delivery of calves, the trapping of foxes, the swollen inflamed eyes of myxomatosis. Tony considered asking one of them about the scream, but now they were all intent on the dartboard; they were a team, practising sombrely for a match. 'I know there's an ending that's right for the book,' Di said. 'It's just finding it.'

When they returned to the cottage, amber clouds floated above the sunset. The horizon was the colour of the stone. The field lay quiet and chill. Di gazed at the cottage, her hands light on the wall. After a while he thought of asking why, but her feelings might be too delicate, too elusive. She would tell him if she could.

They made love beneath the low dark beams. Afterwards he lay in her on their quilt, gazing out at the dimming field. The tree was heavy with gathering darkness; a sheep bleated sleepily. Tony felt peaceful, in harmony. But Di was moving beneath him. 'Don't squash,' she said. As she lay beside him he felt her going into herself, looking for her story. At the moment she didn't dare risk the lure of peace.

When he awoke the room was gloomy. Di lay face upturned, mouth slackly open. Outside the ground hissed with rain beneath a low grey sky; the walls of the room streamed with the shadows of water.

He felt dismally oppressed. He had hoped to paint today.

Now he imagined himself and Di hemmed in by the rain, struggling with their baulks beneath the low beams, wandering irritably about the small rooms, among the fat mock-leather furniture and stray electric fires. He knew Di hoped this book would make her more than just another children's novelist, but it couldn't while he was in the way.

Suddenly he glimpsed the landscape. All the field glowed sultry green. He saw how the dark sky and even the dark framing room were necessary to call forth the sullen glow. Perhaps he could paint that glimpse. After a while he kissed Di awake. She'd wanted to be woken early.

After breakfast she reread *The Song of the Trees*. She turned over the last page of the penultimate chapter and stared at the blank table beneath. At last she pushed herself away from the table and began to pace shortly. Tony tried to keep out of her way. When his own work was frustrated she seemed merely an irritation; he was sure she must feel the same of him. 'I'm going out for a walk,' she called, opening the front door. He didn't offer to walk with her. He knew she was searching for her conclusion.

When the rain ceased he carried his painting materials outside. For a moment he wished he had music. But they couldn't have transported the stereo system, and their radio was decrepit. As he left the cottage he glanced back at Di's flowers, massed minutely in vases.

The grey sky hung down, trapping light in ragged flourishes of white cloud. Distant trees were smudges of mist; the greens of the field merged into a dark glow. On the near side of the fence the path unfurled innumerable leaves, oppressive in their dark intricacy, heavy with raindrops. Even the raindrops were relentlessly green. Metallic chimes and chirrs of birds surrounded him, as did a thick rich smell of earth.

Only the wall of the garden held back the green. The heavy jagged stones were a response to the landscape. He could paint that, the rough texture of stone, the amber stone spattered with darker ruggedness, opposing the overpoweringly lush green. But it wasn't what he'd hoped to paint, and it didn't seem likely to make him much money.

Di liked his paintings. At his first exhibition she'd sought him out to tell him so; that was how they'd met. Her first book was just beginning to earn royalties, she had been working on her second. Before they were married he'd begun to illustrate her work.

If exhibiting wasn't too lucrative, illustrating books was less so. He knew Di felt uneasy as the breadwinner; sometimes he felt frustrated that he couldn't earn them more – the inevitable castration anxiety. That was another reason why she wanted *The Song of the Trees* to sell well: to promote his work. She wanted his illustrations to be as important as the writing.

He liked what there was of the book. He felt his paintings could complement the prose; they'd discussed ways of setting out the pages. The story was about the last dryads of a forest, trapped among the remaining trees by a fire that had sprung from someone's cigarette. As they watched picnickers sitting on blackened stumps amid the ash, breaking branches from the surviving trees, leaving litter and matches among them, the dryads realised they must escape before the next fire. Though it was unheard of, they managed to relinquish the cool green peace of the trees and pass through the clinging dead ash to the greenery beyond. They coursed through the greenery, seeking welcoming trees. But the book was full of their tribulations: a huge grim oak-dryad who drove them away from the saplings he protected; willow dryads who let them go deep into their forest, but only because they would distract the dark thick-voiced spirit of a swamp; glittering birch-dryads, too cold and aloof to bear; morose hawthorns, whose flowers farted at the dryads, in case they were animals come to chew the leaves.

He could tell Di loved writing the book – perhaps too much so, for she'd thought it would produce its own ending. But she had been baulked for weeks. She wanted to write an ending that satisfied her totally, she was determined not to fake anything. He knew she hoped the book might appeal to adults too. 'Maybe it needs peace,' she'd said at last, and that had brought them to the cottage. Maybe she was right. This was only their third day, she had plenty of time.

As he mused the sluggish sky parted. Sunlight spilled over an edge of cloud. At once the greens that had merged into green emerged again, separating: a dozen greens, two dozen. Dots of flowers brightened over the field, colours filled the raindrops piercingly. He saw the patterns at once: almost a mandala. The clouds were whiter now, fragmented by blue; the sky was rolling open from the horizon. He began to mix colours. Surely the dryads must have passed through such a landscape.

The patterns were emerging on his canvas when, beyond the field, someone screamed.

It wasn't Di. He was sure it wasn't a woman's voice. It was the voice he'd heard yesterday, but more outraged still; it sounded as if it were trying to utter something too dreadful for language. The hills swallowed its echoes at once, long before his heart stopped pounding loudly.

As he tried to breathe in calm, he realised what was odd about the scream. It had sounded almost as much like an echo as its reiteration in the hills: louder, but somehow lacking a source. It reminded him – yes, of the echo that sometimes precedes a loud sound-source on a record.

Just an acoustic effect. But that hardly explained the scream itself. Someone playing a joke? Someone trying to frighten the intruders at the cottage? The local simpleton? An animal in a trap, perhaps, for his memory of the scream contained little that sounded human. Someone was watching him.

He turned sharply. Beyond the nearby path, at the far side of the road, stood a clump of trees. The watcher was hiding among them; Tony could sense him there – he'd almost glimpsed him skulking hurriedly behind the trunks. He felt instinctively that the lurker was a man.

Was it the man who'd screamed? No, he hadn't had time to make his way round the edge of the field. Perhaps he had been drawn by the scream. Or perhaps he'd come to spy on the strangers. Tony stared at the trees, waiting for the man to betray his presence, but couldn't stare long; the trunks were vibrating restlessly, incessantly – heat-haze, of course, though it looked somehow odder. Oh, let the man spy if he wanted to. Maybe he'd venture closer to look at Tony's work, as people did. But when Tony rested from his next burst of painting, he could tell the man had gone.

Soon he saw Di hurrying anxiously down the road. Of course, she must have heard the scream. 'I'm all right, love,' he called.

'It was the same, wasn't it? Did you see what it was?'

'No. Maybe it's children. Playing a joke.'

She wasn't reassured so easily. 'It sounded like a man,' she said. She gazed at his painting. 'That *is* good,' she said, and wandered into the cottage without mentioning her book. He knew she wasn't going in to write.

The scream had worried her more than she'd let him see. Her anxiety lingered even now she knew he was unharmed. Something else to hinder her book, he thought irritably. He couldn't paint now, but at least he knew what remained to be painted.

He sat at the kitchen table while she cooked a shepherd's pie in the range. Inertia hung oppressively about them. 'Do you want to go to the pub later?' he said.

'Maybe. I'll see.'

He gazed ahead at the field in the window, the cooling tree; branches swayed a little behind the glass. In the kitchen something trembled – heat over the electric stove. Di was reaching for the teapot with one hand, lifting the kettle with the other; the steaming spout tilted above her bare leg. Tony stood up, mouth opening – but she'd put the kettle down. 'It's all right,' he answered her frown, as he scooped up spilled sugar from the table.

She stood at the range. 'Maybe the pub might help us to relax,' he said.

'I don't want to relax! That's no use!' She turned too quickly, and overbalanced towards the range. Her bare arm was going to rest on the metal that quivered with heat. She pushed herself back from the wall, barely in time. 'You see what I mean?' she demanded.

'What's the matter? Clumsiness isn't like you.'

'Stop watching me, then. You make me nervous.'

'Hey, you can't just blame me.' How would she have felt if she had been spied on earlier? There was more wrong with her than her book and her irrationally lingering worry about him, he was sure. Sometimes she had what seemed to be psychic glimpses. 'Is it the cottage that's wrong?' he said.

'No, I like the cottage.'

'The area, then? The field?'

She came to the table, to saw bread with a carving-knife; the cottage lacked a bread-knife. 'I like it here. It's probably just me,' she said, musing about something.

The kettle sizzled, parched. 'Bloody clean simplicity,' she said. She disliked electric stoves. She moved the kettle to a cold ring and turned back. The point of the carving-knife thrust over the edge of the table. Her turn would impale her thigh on the blade.

Tony snatched the knife back. The blade and the wood of the table seemed to vibrate for a moment. He must have jarred the table. Di was staring rather abstractedly at the knife. 'That's three,' he said. 'You'll be all right now.'

During dinner she was abstracted. Once she said, 'I really like this cottage, you know. I really do.' He didn't try to reach her. After dinner he said, 'Look, I'm sorry if I've been distracting you,' but she shook her head, hardly listening. They didn't seem to be perceiving each other very well.

He was washing up when she said 'My God.' He glanced anxiously at her. She was staring up at the beams. 'Of course. Of course,' she said, reaching for her notebook. She pushed it away at once and hurried upstairs. Almost immediately he heard her begin typing.

He tried to paint, until darkness began to mix with his colours. He stood gazing as twilight collected in the field. The typewriter chattered. He felt rather unnecessary, out of place. He must buy some books in Camside tomorrow. He felt restless, a little resentful. 'I'm going down to the pub for a while,' he called. The typewriter's bell rang, rang again.

The pub was surrounded by jeeps, sports cars, floridly painted vans. Crowds of young people pressed close to the tables, on stools, on the floor; they shouted over each other, laughed, rolled cigarettes. One was passing around a sketchbook, but Tony didn't feel confident enough to introduce himself. A few of the older people doggedly practised darts, the rest surrounded Tony at the bar. He chatted about the weather and the countryside, listened to prices of grain. He hoped he'd have a chance to ask about the scream.

He was slowing in the middle of his second pint when the barman said, 'One of the new ones, aren't you?'

'Yes, that's right.' On an impulse he said loudly enough for the people around him to hear: 'We're in the cottage across the field from Ploughman's Path.'

The man didn't move hurriedly to serve someone else. Nobody gasped, nobody backed away from Tony. Well, that was encouraging. 'Are you liking it?' the barman said.

'Very much. There's just one odd thing.' Now was his chance. 'We keep hearing someone screaming across the field.'

Even then the room didn't fall silent. But it was as if he'd broken a taboo; people withdrew slightly from him, some of them seemed resentful. Three women suddenly excused themselves from different groups at the bar, as if he were threatening to become offensive. 'It'll be an animal caught in a trap,' the barman said.

'I suppose so.' He could see the man didn't believe it either.

The barman was staring at him. 'Weren't you with a girl yesterday?'

'She's back at the cottage.'

Everyone nearby looked at Tony. When he glanced at them, they looked away. 'You want to be sure she's safe,' the barman muttered, and hurried to fill flourished glasses. Tony gulped down his beer, cursing his imagination, and almost ran to the car.

Above the skimming patch of lit tarmac moths ignited; a rabbit froze, then leapt. Discovered trees rushed out of the dark, to be snatched back at once by the night. The light bleached the leaves, the rushing tunnels of boles seemed subterraneously pale. The wide night was still. He could hear nothing but the hum of the car. Above the hills hung enormous dim clouds, grey as rocks.

He could see Di as he hurried up the path. Her head was silhouetted on the curtain; it leaned at an angle against the back of the settee. He fumbled high in the porch for the hidden key. Her eyes were closed, her mouth was loosely open. Her typescript lay at her feet.

She was blinking, smiling at him. He could see both needed effort; her eyes were red, she looked depressed – she always did when she'd finished a book. 'See what you think of it,' she said, handing him the pages. Beneath her attempt at a professional's impersonality he thought she was offering the chapter to him shyly as a young girl.

Emerging defeated from a patch of woodland, the dryads saw a cottage across a field. It stood in the still light, peaceful as the evening. They could feel the peace filling its timbers: not a green peace but a warmth, stillness, stability. As they drew nearer they saw an old couple within. The couple had worked hard for their peace; now they'd achieved it here. Tony knew they were himself and Di. One by one the dryads passed gratefully into the dark wood of the beams, the doors.

He felt oddly embarrassed. When he managed to look at her he could only say, 'Yes, it's good. You've done it.'

'Good,' she said. 'I'm glad.' She was smiling peacefully now.

As they climbed the stairs she said, 'If we have children they'll be able to help me too. They can criticise.'

She hoped the book would let them afford children. 'Yes, they will,' he said.

The scream woke him. For a moment he thought he'd dreamed it, or had cried out in his sleep. But the last echo was caught in the hills. Faint as it was, he could feel its intolerable horror, its despair.

He lay blinking at the sunlight. The white-painted walls shone. Di hadn't woken; he was glad. The scream throbbed in his brain. Today he must find out what it was.

After breakfast he told Di he was going into Camside. She was still depressed after completing the book; she looked drained. She didn't offer to accompany him. She stood at the garden wall, watching him blindly, dazzled by the sun. 'Be careful driving,' she called.

The clump of trees opposite the end of the path was quivering. Was somebody hiding behind the trunks? Tony frowned at her. 'Do you feel –' but he didn't want to alarm her unnecessarily '– anything? Anything odd?'

'What sort of thing?' But he was wondering whether to tell her when she said, 'I like this place. Don't spoil it.'

He went back to her. 'What will you do while I'm out?'

'Just stay in the cottage. I want to read through the book. Why are you whispering?' He smiled at her, shaking his head. The sense of someone watching had faded, though the tree-trunks still quivered.

Plushy white-and-silver layers of cloud sailed across the blue sky. He drove the fifteen miles to Camside, a slow roller-coaster ride between green quilts spread easily over the hills. Turned earth displayed each shoot on the nearer fields, trees met over the roads and parted again.

Camside was wholly the colours of rusty sand; similar stone

framed the wide glass of the library. Mullioned windows multiplied reflections. Gardens and walls were thick with flowers. A small river coursed beneath a bridge; in the water, sunlight darted incessantly among pebbles. He parked outside a pub, The Wheatsheaf, and walked back. Next to the library stood an odd squat building of the amber stone, a square block full of small windows whose open casements were like griddles filled with panes; over its door a new plastic sign said *Camside Observer*. The newspaper's files might be useful. He went in.

A girl sat behind a low white Swedish desk; the crimson bell of her desk-lamp clanged silently against the white walls, the amber windowsills. 'Can I help you?'

'I hope so. I'm, I'm doing some research into an area near here, Ploughman's Path. Have you heard of it?'

'Oh, I don't know.' She was glancing away, looking for help to a middle-aged man who had halted in a doorway behind her desk. 'Mr Poole?' she called.

'We've run a few stories about that place,' the man told Tony. 'You'll find them in our files, on microfilm. Next door, in the library.'

'Oh good. Thanks.' But that might mean hours of searching. 'Is there anyone here who knows the background?'

The man frowned, and saw Tony realise that meant Yes. 'The man who handled the last story is still on our staff,' he said. 'But he isn't here now.'

'Will he be here later?'

'Yes, probably. No, I've no idea when.' As Tony left he felt the man was simply trying to prevent his colleague from being pestered.

The library was a long room, spread with sunlight. Sunlight lay dazzling on the glossy tables, cleaved shade among the bookcases; a trolley overflowed with thrillers and romances. Ploughman's Path? Oh yes – and the librarian showed him a card file that indexed local personalities, events, areas. She snapped up a card for him, as if it were a Tarot's answer. Ploughman's Path: see Victor Hill, *Legendry and Customs of the*

Severn Valley. 'And there's something on microfilm,' she said, but he was anxious to make sure the book was on the shelf.

It was. It was bound in op-art blues. He carried it to a table; its blues vibrated in the sunlight. The index told him the passage about Ploughman's Path covered six pages. He riffled hastily past photographs of standing stones, a trough in the binding full of breadcrumbs, a crushed jagged-legged fly. Ploughman's Path –

'Why the area bounding Ploughman's Path should be dogged by ill luck and tragedy is not known. Folk living in the cottage nearby have sometimes reported hearing screams produced by no visible agency. Despite the similarity of this to banshee legends, no such legend appears to have grown up locally. But Ploughman's Path, and the area bounding it furthest from the cottage (see map), has been so often visited by tragedy and misfortune that local folk dislike to even mention the name, which they fear will bring bad luck.'

Furthest from the cottage. Tony relaxed. So long as the book said so, that was all right. And the last line told him why they'd behaved uneasily at the Farmer's Rest. He read on, his curiosity unmixed now with apprehension.

But good Lord, the area was unlucky. Rumours of Roman sacrifices were only its earliest horrors. As the history of the place became more accurately documented, the tragedies grew worse. A gallows set up within sight of the cottage, so that the couple living there must watch their seven-year-old daughter hanged for theft; it had taken her hours to die. An old woman accused of witchcraft by gossip, set on fire and left to burn alive on the path. A mute child who'd fallen down an old well: coping-stones had fallen on him, breaking his limbs and hiding him from searchers – years later his skeleton had been found. A baby caught in an animal trap. God, Tony thought. No wonder he'd heard screams.

A student was using the microfilm reader. Tony went back to the *Observer* building. A pear-shaped red-faced man leaned against the wall, chatting to the receptionist; he wore a tweedy pork-pie hat, a blue shirt and waistcoat, tweed trousers. 'Watch out, here's trouble,' he said as Tony entered.

'Has he come in yet?' Tony asked the girl. 'The man who knows about Ploughman's Path?'

'What's your interest?' the red-faced man demanded.

'I'm staying in the cottage near there. I've been hearing odd things. Cries.'

'Have you now.' The man pondered, frowning. 'Well, you're looking at the man who knows,' he decided to say, thumping his chest. 'Roy Burley. Burly Roy, that's me. Don't you know me? Don't you read our paper? Time you did, then.' He snatched an *Observer* from a rack and stuffed it into Tony's hand.

'You want to know about the path, eh? It's all up here.' He tapped his hat. 'I'll tell you what, though, it's a hot day for talking. Do you fancy a drink? Tell old Puddle I'll be back soon,' he told the girl.

He thumped on the door of The Wheatsheaf. 'They'll open up. They know me here.' At last a man reluctantly opened the door, glancing discouragingly at Tony. 'It's all right, Bill, don't look so bloody glum,' Roy Burley said. 'He's a friend of mine.'

A girl set out beer mats; her radio sang that everything was beautiful, in its own way. Roy Burley bought two pints and vainly tried to persuade Bill to join them. 'Get that down you,' he told Tony. 'The only way to start work. You'd think they could do without me over the road, the way some of the buggers act. But they soon start screaming if they think my copy's going to be late. They'd like to see me out, some of them. Unfortunately for them, I've got friends. There I am,' he said, poking a thick finger into the newspaper: *The Countryside This Week*, by Countryman. 'And there, and there.' *Social Notes*, by A. Guest. *Entertainments*, by D. Plainman. 'What's your line of business?' he demanded.

'I'm an artist, a painter.'

'Ah, the painters always come down here. And the advertising people. I'll tell you, the other week we had a photographer –'

By the time it was his round Tony began to suspect he was just an excuse for beers. 'You were going to tell me about the screams,' he said when he returned to the table.

The man's eyes narrowed warily. 'You've heard them. What do you think they are?'

'I was reading about the place earlier,' Tony said, anxious to win his confidence. 'I'm sure all those tragedies must have left an imprint somehow. A kind of recording. If there are ghosts, I think that's what they are.'

'That's right.' Roy Burley's eyes relaxed. 'I've always thought that. There's a bit of science in that, it makes sense. Not like some of the things these spiritualists try to sell.'

Tony opened his mouth to head him off from the next anecdote: too late. 'We had one of them down here, trying to tell us about Ploughman's Path. A spiritualist or a medium, same thing. Came expecting us all to be yokels, I shouldn't wonder. The police weren't having any, so he tried it on us. Murder brings these mediums swarming like flies, so I've heard tell.'

'What murder?' Tony said, confused.

'I thought you read about it.' His eyes had narrowed again. 'Oh, you read the book. No, it wouldn't be in there, too recent.' He gulped beer; everything is beautiful, the radio sang. 'Why, it was about the worst thing that ever happened at Ploughman's Path. I've seen pictures of what Jack the Ripper did, but this was worse. They talk about people being flayed alive, but – Christ. Put another in here, Bill.'

He half-emptied the refilled glass. 'They never caught him. I'd have stopped him, I can tell you,' he said in vague impotent fury. 'The police didn't think he was a local man, because there wasn't any repetition. He left no clues, nobody saw him. At least, not what he looked like. There was a family picnicking in the field the day before the murder, they said they kept feeling there was someone watching. He must have been waiting to catch someone alone.

'I'll tell you the one clever suggestion this medium had. These picnickers heard the scream, what you called the recording. He thought maybe the screams were what attracted the maniac there.'

Attracted him there. That reminded Tony of something, but the beer was heavy on his mind. 'What else did the medium have to say?'

'Oh, all sorts of rubbish. You know, this mystical stuff. Seeing patterns everywhere, saying everything is a pattern.'

'Yes?'

'Oh yes,' Roy Burley said irritably. 'He didn't get that one past me, though. If everything's a pattern it has to include all the horror in the world, doesn't it? Things like this murder? That shut him up for a bit. Then he tried to say things like that may be necessary too, to make up the pattern. These people,' he said with a gesture of disgust, 'you can't talk to them.'

Tony bought him another pint, restraining himself to a half. 'Did he have any ideas about the screams?'

'God, I can't remember. Do you really want to hear that rubbish? You wouldn't have liked what he said, let me tell you. He didn't believe in your recording idea.' He wiped his frothy lips sloppily. 'He came here a couple of years after the murder,' he reluctantly answered Tony's encouraging gaze. 'He'd read about the tragedies. He held a three-day vigil at Ploughman's Path, or something. Wouldn't it be nice to have that much time to waste? He heard the screams, but – this is what I said you wouldn't like – he said he couldn't feel any trace of the tragedies at all.'

'I don't understand.'

'Well, you know these people are shuppposed to be senshitive to sush things.' When he'd finished laughing at himself he said 'Oh, he had an explanation, he was full of them. He tried to tell the police and me that the real tragedy hadn't happened yet. He wanted us to believe he could see it in the future. Of course he couldn't say what or when. Do you know what he tried to make out? That there was something so awful in the future it was echoing back somehow, a sort of ghost in reverse. All the tragedies were just echoes, you see. He even made out the place was trying to make this final thing happen, so it could get rid of it at last. It had to make the worst thing possible happen, to purge itself. That was where the traces of the tragedies had gone – the psychic energy, he called it. The place had converted all that energy, to help it make the thing happen. Oh, he was a real comedian.'

'But what about the screams?'

'Same kind of echo. Haven't you ever heard an echo on a record before you hear the sound? He tried to say the screams were like that, coming back from the future. He was entertaining, I'll give him that. He had all sorts of charts, he'd worked out some kind of numerical pattern, the frequency of the tragedies or something. Didn't impress me. They're like statistics, those things, you can make them mean anything.' His eyes had narrowed, gazing inward. 'I ended up laughing at him. He went off very upset. Well, I had to get rid of him, I'd better things to do than listen to him. It wasn't my fault he was killed,' he said angrily, 'whatever some people may say.'

'Why, how was he killed?'

'Oh, he went back to Ploughman's Path. If he was so upset he shouldn't have been driving. There were some children playing near the path. He must have meant to chase them away, but he lost control of the car, crashed at the end of the path. His legs were trapped and he caught fire. Of course he could have fitted that into his pattern,' he mused. 'I suppose he'd have said that was what the third scream meant.'

Tony started. He fought back the shadows of beer, of the pub. 'How do you mean, the third scream?'

'That was to do with his charts. He'd heard three screams in his vigil. He'd worked out that three screams meant it was time for a tragedy. He tried to show me, but I wasn't looking.

What's the matter? Don't be going yet, it's my round. What's up, how many screams have you heard?'

'I don't know,' Tony blurted. 'Maybe I dreamt one.' As he hurried out he saw Roy Burley picking up his abandoned beer, saying, 'Aren't you going to finish this?'

It was all right. There was nothing to worry about, he'd just better be getting back to the cottage. The key groped clumsily for the ignition. The rusty yellow of Camside rolled back, rushed by green. Tony felt as if he were floating in a stationary car, as the road wheeled by beneath him – as if he were sitting in the front stalls before a cinema screen, as the road poured through the screen, as the bank of a curve hurtled at him: look out! Nearly. He slowed. No need to take risks. But his mind was full of the memory of someone watching from the trees, perhaps drawn there by the screams.

Puffy clouds lazed above the hills. As the Farmer's Rest whipped by Tony glimpsed the cottage and the field, laid out minutely below; the trees at Ploughman's Path were a tight band of green. He skidded into the side road, fighting the wheel; the road seemed absurdly narrow. Scents of blossoms billowed thickly at him. A few birds sang elaborately, otherwise the passing countryside was silent, deserted, weighed down by heat.

The trunks of the trees at the end of Ploughman's Path were twitching nervously, incessantly. He squeezed his eyes shut. Only heat-haze. Slow down. Nearly home now.

He slammed the car door, which sprang open. Never mind. He ran up the path and thrust the gate back, breaking its latch. The door of the cottage was ajar. He halted in the front room. The cottage seemed full of his harsh panting.

Di's typescript was scattered over the carpet. The dark chairs sat fatly; one lay on its side, its fake leather ripped. Beside it a small object glistened red. He picked it up, staining his fingers. Though it was thick with blood he recognised Di's wedding ring.

When he rushed out after searching the cottage he saw the

trail at once. As he forced his way through the fence, sobbing dryly, barbed wire clawed at him. He ran across the field, stumbling and falling, towards Ploughman's Path. The discoloured grass of the trail painted his trouser-cuffs and hands red. The trees of Ploughman's Path shook violently, with terror or with eagerness. The trail touched their trunks, leading him beneath the foliage to what lay on the path.

It was huge. More than anything else it looked like a tattered cut-out silhouette of a woman's body. It gleamed red beneath the trees; its torso was perhaps three feet wide. On the width of the silhouette's head two eyes were arranged neatly.

The scream ripped the silence of the path, an outraged cry of horror beyond words. It startled him into stumbling forward. He felt numb and dull. His mind refused to grasp what he was seeing; it was like nothing he'd ever seen. There was most of the head, in the crotch of a tree. Other things dangled from branches.

His lips seemed glued together. Since reaching the path he had made no sound. He hadn't screamed, but he'd heard himself scream. At last he recognised that all the screams had been his voice.

He began to turn about rapidly, staring dull-eyed, seeking a direction in which he could look without being confronted with horror. There was none. He stood aimlessly, staring down near his feet, at a reddened gag.

As all the trees quivered like columns of water he heard movement behind him.

Though he had no will to live, it took him a long time to turn. He knew the pattern had reached its completion, and he was afraid. He had to close his eyes before he could turn, for he could still hear the scream he was about to utter.

Dark Wings

by

FRITZ LEIBER

Fritz Leiber (1910–) has acted in films, and was minister of two missionary churches in New Jersey, but it's his writing which has made him deservedly famous, and has earned him five Hugo Awards and two Nebulas. Many of his excellent short science fiction stories are included in The Best Of Fritz Leiber. *Besides inventing the term 'sword and sorcery' he has written some of the most enjoyable stories in that vein, his series about Fafhrd and the Grey Mouser. Even better than his science fiction novels is* Conjure Wife, *one of the few completely successful novels of supernatural horror. He recently completed a new horror novel,* The Pale Brown Thing.

He is a master of the short story of modern supernatural terror, especially in an urban setting – often San Francisco, where he lives. His collections Night's Black Agents, Shadows With Eyes, *and* Night Monsters *contain many of his best; here is a new and most disturbing example.*

Rose locked the stout screen door of heavy mesh behind them, then closed and double locked the solid door, put on the chain, shot the three bolts (high, medium, and low) and squatting somewhat precariously on her high heels, tugged at the door's hinged buttress-bar to free it from its clamp.

Vi said mischievously, 'Now we're locked in for the night,' but when Rose looked up startledly, explained, 'Just the tag line of one of the standard ghost stories,' and remarked, 'You really do things thoroughly.'

'A girl can't be too careful,' Rose stated, tugging some more. 'There have been three burglaries since I moved here a year ago, two muggings just outside the lobby, and one attempted rape. Oh blast! – this always sticks. I won't let a strange man inside my apartment unless the manager's with him – she's a woman. Ow! – now I've pinched my finger.' She winced and sucked it.

'Par for the Village,' Vi said. 'Here, let me.'

She knelt effortlessly, one leg stretched out behind, her back straight, freed the buttress-bar with a controlled jerk, and forced its end into the socket in the floor-plate. There was a harsh, grating, rather high-pitched scrape and click. Rose winced again.

Vi said, 'That sort of sound sets my teeth on edge too. But why do you shut your eyes?'

Rose replied, 'I've got synesthesia – I see sounds, hear colours, that sort of thing. My psychiatrist says I'm a classic case. She says most people only imagine the colours, but I actually see them. The bar was a lilac flash, my pinched finger a bright red one. It didn't break the skin, though,' she announced after studying it closely. 'Come on, Vi, let's compare some more. There really wasn't a proper mirror in Nathan's,' and rather shyly taking the other young woman's hand, she led her to a large mirror that made up one third of the inner wall of the pleasantly furnished, medium-size one-room apartment.

'It really is remarkable,' she said softly after a bit.

'As we already decided at Nathans,' Vi reminded her, but her voice was a shade awe-struck too.

Anyone studying the two faces side by side, as they were now, would have concluded that beyond the shadow of a doubt these two were identical twins. Their figures were alike – slender, petite. Vi was two inches shorter – her flats – but Rose toed off her shoes and that difference vanished. Rose wore a knee-length blue dress that buttoned down the front and her blonde hair in a page-boy bob that brushed her shoulders. Vi, a trim blue slack suit, a shirt of paler blue, and her blonde hair cut short, almost *en brosse*. They looked like one of those delightful, genetically impossible sets of boy-girl identical twins from Shakespeare, only in this case Violet was Sebastian and Rose, Viola.

Rose said, 'Blue is my favourite colour.'

Vi said, 'So is mine.'

Rose said, 'I had my appendix out a year ago.'

Vi responded, 'They took mine too – year and a half.'

Rose said, 'My first pet was a kitten named Blackie.'

Vi echoed, 'And so was mine, believe it or not, Little Black.'

Their eyes were getting wider all the time.

Rose continued, almost chanting, 'I have a mole on my left breast.'

Vi grinned, held up a palm, and swiftly unbuttoned her shirt. Rose gave a start, drew off a little, and watched uneasily in the mirror. Vi, studying her sidewise, pulled down her paler blue singlet of ribbed lightweight cotton, exposing her small, attractive breasts, a dark brown mole on the inner curve of her right one.

She said insistently with an odd undercurrent of amusement, 'For a moment you were scared I was a man after all, got in past your locks. Well, weren't you?'

'Well, yes,' Rose admitted uncomfortably, blushing, then said eagerly, 'But you do have a mole, and on your left breast too.'

'Wrong, right,' Vi corrected. 'You're looking in the mirror, which reverses. We're mirror-image twins, like all identicals. Now, how about you?' She smiled.

'Oh, yes,' Rose said apologetically, quickly beginning to fumble at the neck of her dress. 'There's a tiny hook and eye here. I can never –'

'Let me,' Vi said coolly, still smiling, and undid it, then went on efficiently to unbutton the top of the blue dress. Rose was wearing a dark blue brassiere. Vi's eyebrows lifted.

Rose explained hurriedly, 'Mother – I mean my foster mother got me to always wearing one. I still don't ever wear pantyhose,' as she took over, saying, 'This hooks in front. With my all-thumbs fingers I never can work the ones that hook behind. There. See the mole?'

The touch of awe briefly returned to Vi's voice as she said, 'And to think that two hours ago neither of us knew we had a sister, let alone an identical twin.'

Rose said, 'Vi, why do you suppose our foster mothers never told us about each other?'

Vi chuckled harshly. 'Mine would never have told me anything nice. She hated me, because foster papa liked me – and more and more the more I grew. Dig?'

'Oh,' Rose said feebly, hooking her brassiere again. 'My foster father was sort of weak and timid. Mother – my foster mother, I mean, ran everything, especially me. She smothered me with love, very possessive and jealous, and wanted me to be like her exactly. I guess that's why she never told me about you. You'd have been a rival. You might have taken me away from her.'

Vi's chuckle was bitter, though the undercurrent of distant amusement was still there. 'The wonder is they told us our right birthdays.'

'So we could find out tonight they were the same,' Rose took up. 'Just think, Vi, in three weeks we can have a birthday party together – two Children of the Moon.'

'That's right, dear sister, two Cancers, the dark sign,' Vi agreed, giving Rose's waist a brief squeeze with one arm as she moved away from the mirror towards the daybed with its light Paisley spread and scatter of gay pillows.

'Gee, it's so strange to have someone calling me sister,' Rose said, smiling in wonder.

'Not just someone,' Vi reminded her, grinning mischievously back over her shoulder.

'That's what I mean,' Rose protested, 'a sister calling me sister . . . sister darling,' she added, getting a lump in her throat as she said the two words.

Vi nodded as she looked the bookcase over and then studied more closely the dozen volumes between collie-dog bookends on the low table in front of the daybed, as she sat down on it.

'You have a lot of books,' she observed.

'I'm in the publishing business,' Rose explained. 'That is, I make indexes for a man who is. Say, would you like some more coffee? I'm going to make some,' she continued, opening some light folding shutters in the nook that also held the bathroom door and revealing a small refrigerator top, electric stove, and sink all in line with cupboards above and below.

'That would be fine,' Vi said. 'I dance for a man who does TV toothpaste commercials. I'm the third vampire. We dance slow motion in filmy negligees that float out very artistically all over a huge bathroom, baring our teeth. Then Dracula comes in, flashing *his* teeth, in a black dressing gown, a head taller than any of us and very thin, and we make love to him with our large dark liquid eyes, flashing our teeth some more, and he holds up the toothpaste we all four use as (in the newest version) we come together for a group tooth-baring, facing camera. Actually he's gay. And then four evenings a week I have my ballet classes.'

'Why, I've seen that commercial,' Rose said, filling and putting on the stove the silvery hemisphere of the teakettle. 'But you don't look like you. Your hair –'

'– is a long black wig,' Vi interrupted. 'And then those three-quarter-inch eyelashes do something to my face. Not to mention all that blood-red lipstick, which they varnish on so it won't smudge our teeth. It takes us fifteen minutes to get it all off afterwards. But not Dracula – the make-up boy is his very special friend. Say, these books are interesting – more twin identicalities.' And she read off, '*The Plays of Shakespeare, Newman on Twins, Fear of Flying, Women and Madness* by Phyllis Chesler, *The Wind in the Willows*, Jung's *The Archetypes, Animus and Anima*, by Joan S. Rosenbloom, M.D. – that's one I don't have –'

'She's my psychiatrist. My firm published it. I did the index,' Rose said proudly, sitting down on the daybed two feet from Vi, between her and the casement windows, which were open a third of the way and locked in that position. Traffic sounds floated in irregularly and the faint steady thud of a hi-fi's woofer. 'You know the animus, of course, if you've read Jung – the male self that haunts and inspires and sometimes terrifies each of us women, overshadowing the shadow. The equivalent of the anima in a man.' An intense look came into Rose's face, contracting her soft brow. She looked a little like a blonde Barbi doll being very fierce. 'I'd like to be some man's anima, some young stud's,' she said with surprising venom. 'I'd terrorise him. I'd make him suffer.'

'Think you'd be up to it?' Vi asked her playfully, but with the distance again, her chuckle throaty. 'Like your foster mother terrorised her husband, eh? But worse than that, of course.'

'I'm not sure,' Rose confessed flusteredly, her face relaxing. 'All the archetypes can be pretty frightening sometimes, just to think about. But to actually be one . . .' She hesitated, then blurted out, 'You know, Vi, I've sometimes imagined they really existed. The archetypes, I mean. Not just in my mind, but somehow outside where I might see and touch them.'

'Why not?' Vi asked lazily yet soothingly, apparently still playful. 'That's how everything exists – outside. Nothing's just in the mind and nowhere else. Witches are real people, aren't they? Then why not demons and other so-called spirits? Jesus was a real person, wasn't he? – but also God. Then why not a real Jungian shadow moving around, a real anima? And a real animus.'

There was a sudden rushing, whirring sound and something struck one of the black casement windows with a jar and rattled the pane sharply. Rose started to clutch at Vi, then checked herself, her face twisted towards the night.

'Relax,' Vi said with a gentle chuckle. 'That was just a bird.

A lost and mixed-up pigeon, probably.'

'If it had been a pigeon we'd have seen a flash of white. Did you?' Rose said rapidly, breathily. 'Or a dove. They're white too. Some of them nest here, under the eaves.'

'There are black pigeons – and black doves too, I suppose,' Vi said. 'Relax.'

'Yes, and black hawks and eagles ... and other things. Besides, that was too heavy for a dove or pigeon.'

Vi sat up a little, smiling with a mixture of amusement and tenderness, and slowly reached out a hand, saying, 'A black eagle in Manhattan! What would it do, Rose? Fly in ominous circles over Wall Street?' but before her fingers quite touched Rose there came a sudden fluttering whistle which swiftly grew louder and shriller. Rose got up hurriedly and crossed to the kitchenette, her hands ahead of her and her eyes closed or rather almost closed, like a person walking into a dusty wind.

'What's the matter, sis? Are you getting more lilac flashes?' Vi asked solicitously, watching her.

Rose lifted the steam-jetting kettle off the heating element. The whistling quickly died.

'Yes, I was – bright ones that hurt,' she answered sharply and a shade defiantly, reaching down a brown jar of coffee crystals out of the cupboard. 'They started green, then went through blue to violet as the pitch rose. With streaks of red – the pain.'

'I'm truly sorry,' Vi said. 'That must be very strange and frightening, what you have – and also very painful, your ...?'

'Synesthesia,' Rose supplied. 'How big a teaspoon do you take? Level, mounded, or heaping?'

'It doesn't matter –' Vi began. Then, 'No – heaping.'

Rose brought the two steaming mugs over and set them on the table. 'Watch out,' she said rather huffily, 'they're hot.' Suddenly her eyes flashed and she grinned like a naughty girl. 'Suppose I put a little brandy in them,' she whispered loudly to Vi. 'There's some left from a bottle I bought for Christmas.'

'I think that would be fun,' Vi told her.

Rose's eyes got bigger still with the mischief of it as she fetched and added the brandy, a pony apiece and then a little more at Vi's suggestion. They took a burning, aromatic, eye-moistening swallow together, looking at each other, and Rose confessed, 'I got a little mad when I got scared and you just told me to relax. But now I'm feeling wonderful.'

'And so am I,' Vi assured her. 'What is that mournful night sound?' she asked, eyeing the windows.

'Oh, that's the doves,' Rose said. 'Whatever it was must have waked them up. They nest under the eaves, as I told you, and this apartment is right under them.'

'I'd think you'd be afraid of someone getting in that way,' Vi suggested, serious eyed. 'You know, down off the roof, around the eaves, and in through the windows. Though he'd have to have a good head for climbing.'

'Don't think I'm not,' Rose assured her aggressively. 'But they've each got a hook and also a bolt bar which can't either be unfastened from the outside when I leave them partly open in warm weather like this.'

'That sounds completely safe,' Vi said neutrally, drinking her coffee royale.

Rose took a big swallow of hers and said, 'I know you think I'm silly, Vi, for being so scared and fussing so about my locks and bolts. But really, Vi, if anyone ever got in and raped me, I know I'd die, or else go crazy.'

'You think so now,' Vi said softly and bitterly, eyeing the floor. 'Your locks and bolts – I think they're sensible.'

'What do you mean?' Rose demanded. Then her eyebrows went up. 'You mean that you . . .?'

Vi nodded.

'Oh, you poor thing,' Rose gasped. 'Oh my God, how horrible, how terribly horrible. How did it happen, Vi? Did someone con his way into your place, get you to take off the chain? Or were you out alone late at night on some dark street? Or –?'

Vi shook her head. 'I was home in my own bed, being a good girl,' she said with a sour smile and wrinkled nostrils. 'I told you that my foster father had a lech for me –'

'Oh my God,' Rose breathed.

'Well, one night when he was drunk – and after getting my foster mother dead drunk, of course – he just came into my bedroom and satisfied it. Afterwards –'

'Didn't you try to fight him off, Vi? Were you so terrified that –?'

'Of course I did and in every dirty way I knew,' Vi said harshly, 'but they weren't dirty enough and he was stronger.'

'Oh my God, Vi, did it hurt?'

'It hurt like hell,' Vi said savagely. 'But even that wasn't as bad as the way he slobbered over me afterwards, telling me how sorry he was. There wasn't even much blood. No, the worst thing was being touched – and not only touched, but invaded – where only you have ever touched yourself before, and then only very gently, very tentatively, almost reverently, a special thing, just like (I suppose) a man touches his –'

'I know, I know,' Rose groaned, rocking back and forth. 'I've dreamed of it.'

'Anywhere else, almost, they have to cut you with a knife to get inside you,' Vi said viciously. 'But there –'

'I know, I know,' Rose echoed herself agonisedly. 'I *hate* to be touched there, even by cloth.'

Vi caught her breath, drank the last of her brandy and coffee, and said in another voice, a more open and even roughly humorous one, 'I'll give the gays this. At least they know what it's like to be raped.'

'How do you mean?' Rose asked, gulping the last of hers.

'Oh come on, Rose,' Vi said impatiently, but with a little grin, 'you've got the books right out there, dear identical: the Masters and Johnson, *The Joys of Sex*, even *Anomalies and Curiosities of Medicine* – you know, that's the only other copy I've ever seen of that oldy besides my own.'

'Yes, I do know how you mean,' Rose admitted, looking

away, 'but really, it's all so horrible and disgusting and frightening. Oh, I don't see how you managed to stand it, Vi.'

'I wasn't asked whether I wanted to,' the other said shortly.

Rose said, 'At least you got back at that horrible beast a little by telling your foster mother?'

Vi replied cynically, 'She'd have been the last one to believe he would ever have had to rape me. She had her own evaluation of Sweet Fourteen.

'Now come on, Rose, it's not so terrible,' Vi continued, 'or rather, yes, it was just that terrible, but it's all over now. It happened long – well, fairly long ago. As for the gays, they're mostly quite charming, or at least funny. The make-up boy I mentioned has breasts, for instance – cute little silicone ones. Of course the nipples are a little small.'

'I don't believe that,' Rose protested, clapping her fingers to her mouth to smother a nervous giggle.

'True, just the same.' Vi settled back and her face got a tight little smile. 'Besides,' she said, breathing deeply, 'I got my own back at my loving father, let me tell you, in my own sweet time and way. After –'

She broke off because there was a repetition of the whirring, rushing sound and again the black pane was jarred and rattled with no flash of white, as if a ragged portion of the night had launched itself down at it, only this time the sounds kept up – there was a frantic beating and loud rapid brushing at the pane and then a series of higher and higher pitched, skirling, inhuman cries.

And this time Rose clutched at once at Vi through the bright magenta flashes that had invaded her eyes.

Her twin clasped her protectively, saying, 'There, there, Rose, it's all right. It's just a bird again, only this time it's somehow caught itself. My God, your heart is pounding. I'm looking over your shoulder straight at the windows and I can't see anything through them or in the space between them, except maybe a sort of black flashing. There, there. I'd better go and try to release the thing. No, let me go, Rose, it's the only way we can make the noise stop.'

Terrified, palms pressed to her ears, Rose watched through slitted, lash-blurred eyes and purple floods as Vi went to the windows and stood before them, a slender blue figure against the big black square they made, turning sideways to thrust a shoulder through the narrow space between them and all that arm and her cropped blonde head and her other arm to the elbow. Between the torturing, skirling cries, which rose in volume, and the beating, which became still more frantic, she heard Vi give a sharp exclamation, then both cries and beatings were receding rapidly, the pitch of the former dropping, and then the sounds were cut off completely, almost abruptly.

In the shocking though very welcome silence that followed, Vi withdrew her upper body from the night and turned around and said, returning towards Rose, 'It was a large black bird I didn't know, some kind of predatory hawk, I'd think, a *raptor*, though certainly not an eagle, perhaps a crow or raven. Its wing was caught under one of the bolt bars. While I was loosing it, it struck me twice with its beak, but –' (She lifted her hand towards her eyes and rotated it) '– it didn't break the skin.'

All this while Rose was staring at her as if hypnotised and without moving a muscle except that her hands dropped slowly away from her ears.

Vi seated herself on the daybed close beside her, between her and the window, and put her arms around the frozen form and pressed her chest against hers firmly and, turning her face sideways so their noses missed, kissed her upon the lips.

A distant foghorn sounded, a car turned a corner far below, a dove mourned, and then time began to move again.

Vi reached for the brandy bottle and the miniature goblet of the pony glass, saying, 'After that fright you need another drink.'

Rose said, as if still half in a dream, 'That was the first time that we ever kissed. Identical twin sisters. Imagine that.'

Vi said companionably, but with her voice a shade brisk,

like that of a nurse, 'Here, drink this down. You need it straight. No, all at once.'

Rose complied, shuddering.

'That's a good girl,' Vi said and kissed her quickly on the corner of the mouth.

After a moment Rose returned the kiss in the same way.

Vi left one arm lightly beside her twin's waist. Her other hand lay against Rose's knee. She asked, 'During that ruckus did you have your synesthesia?'

'Yes, very badly,' Rose replied, wincing in recollection. 'I never had it quite as bad, in fact.'

'What colour were the lights this time?'

'Violet. I never had so much violet before.'

'Perhaps I am responsible for that,' Vi joked with a chuckle. 'My name, you now.'

'Silly,' Rose said indulgently, giving the hand that lay against her knee an affectionate squeeze. Then, more seriously, though still a shade dreamily, 'I wonder if those were our real names from the start. Could be, you know. They're both flower names.'

'Maybe,' Vi said, 'or maybe not. Maybe our real mother never had time to give us any.'

'Do you suppose we're illegitimate?' Rose asked solemnly.

'I'd think so,' Vi replied. 'That's where most foster children come from.'

'But maybe they were married,' Rose said happily, her elbow pressing Vi's hand against her waist. 'Maybe our father died early in the Vietnam War.'

Vi said, frowning a little, 'There's one thing bothers me about your synesthesia.'

'What's that?'

'That I don't have a trace of it. Which is strange, seeing we have so many other twin identicalities.'

Rose said consolingly, 'You probably have some other equally distinguishing peculiarity or ability or trait to match my coloured sounds thing. There's your ballet dancing – how about that? You're terribly graceful and strong and competent-fingered . . . and brave too,' she added, looking over Vi's shoulder at the black windows and remembering the slim blue figure fearlessly thrust between them. 'By comparison, I'm clumsy as a cow.'

'No, a big floppy dog,' Vi decided, running her fingers lazily into the pageboy bob and twice pushing the side of Rose's head – who sketched a bowwow comically and said, 'That's right. And you're a kitty cat.'

'But dancing and finger dexterity and all that are things that are learned,' Vi said more seriously. 'You could develop them too if you practised and exercised instead of sitting inside all day making your indexes – and reading all night.' She nodded towards the bookcase. 'They're not at all like your synesthesia,' she finished regretfully.

'You think that's so great?' Rose challenged lightly. 'You should try it some time. But maybe you've got a mix-up on some other senses.' She pulled away a moment to gesture at the thickest book on the table between the collie bookends – *Anomalies and Curiosities of Medicine*. 'I remember the case of a girl there who heard odours as sounds. Or was it sounds as odours? I forget. Or maybe you've got absolute pitch or are double jointed or –'

'Oh, if you're using *that* book, anything goes,' Vi asserted happily. 'Maybe I've got supernumerary nipples, or a little hairless tail, like that noble European family – I haven't looked today. Or six fingers on each hand – no, five, I just counted. And then there was that woman who had a clitoris four inches long when stimulated.'

'Vi, you're making that one up,' Rose protested, seeming to flush and looking aside.

'Oh, no, I'm not, as you know very well,' Vi laughed, bringing her head around to look her twin straight in the eyes. 'I thought so. Somehow that's the first thing everyone reads.'

Rose squirmed.

Vi grew thoughtful, the distance coming back into her eyes. She mumbled, 'I wonder if that would be the animus – a female with a penis? The grand hermaphrodite. Or would that be the anima? Or neither?' She looked behind her towards the night outside and said more clearly, 'You know, Rose, when I was at that window with that bird, I had the strongest feeling of the presence of one of the archetypes.'

'So did I too!' Rose blurted out tensely. 'It was very scary, something beyond the flashing lights and pain.'

Vi embraced Rose reassuringly, one hand upon her shoulder, the other on her cheek, pressing her other cheek against her own. 'There, there,' she breathed and Rose was comforted.

Vi gave them both a little more brandy and said, 'Remember how you said you'd like to be some man's anima and torture him?'

Rose nodded. 'Though I don't think any more that I'd be up to it.'

'So? Well, I was once my foster father's anima. After he raped me I knew I was going to leave home for good, but I wanted to get my own back at him first – or should I say our own? I got ready to leave – money and clothes, an address in New York – and all the while I watched him like a hawk. For a while he held off from me. He was afraid, of course, he might have got me pregnant. He hadn't – I had my period a week later, though I took care not to let either of them know. A few nights after that he tried the same trick again – getting my foster mother dead drunk and all – but I was ready for him and I kicked him in the balls (I'd kept my shoes on) so that he squealed and fainted.'

Rose breathed, 'My God.'

Vi continued, 'The next couple of days my foster mother kept asking him why he was walking bowlegged and bent over. He said it must be rheumatism inherited from his great grandfather, who'd fought in the Civil War.

'You'd have thought he'd have had enough by then, of course, but he kept trying – men are such fools, or rather they have an endless blind persistence when it comes to *that*. This time he changed his tactics. After he'd put my foster mother to sleep again, he presented me with a dozen red roses and a real diamond ring and the *cutest* black silk peekaboo panties and half-cup brassiere – he even had the right size.

'And this time he'd decided he had to get me drunk too because I was such a smart and worldly little bitch. I played along with it, pretending to get soused with him and promising him that just in a little while longer I'd model the brassiere and panties for him. He kept stumbling around after me in circles. The music throbbed, the lights were low, and every little while I'd dump a little whisky down my neck to make me smell as if I had been drinking.

'Eventually he passed out blotto flat on his face on the floor. I took what cash he had and what more he and his wife had around the house and brought down my bag – it was already packed – and then I hauled down his pants and greased my old toothbrush and rammed it up his ass, bristles first, all the way in.'

Rose gasped, 'My God. *My God!*'

'And then,' Vi finished, 'I scattered the dozen red roses over him and departed that place.'

She took a deep breath and let it out. Rose sat frozen, as if in thought or shock.

Vi asked, 'So how does it feel to have a twin sister who's a criminal, who rips off loose cash and sees that the men she disapproves of get buggered?'

Rose shook herself a little, smiled nervously, and said quickly, 'Oh, no, it feels all right. It's just that my own foster father was so very different. He was very gentle, almost timid with me. I can't remember him ever touching me. He treated me like a little stranger princess. He read me fairy tales and books like *Winnie the Pooh* and *The Borrowers* and *Little Women* and, later on, *Wuthering Heights*. He had poor health and couldn't get good jobs. He would have liked to be a beatnik poet. I thought he was perfect until – but that came later on. No, it was from my foster mother that all the violence came, the things that frightened me and ruled my life.'

'That figures,' Vi said. 'I mean, you said she was possessive and bossy?'

'She was more than that, Vi. She was the power and she was the law. She was almost – My first memory was of her leaning over my bed and smiling down at me fiercely like the sun, bare to the waist and with her arms and breasts thrust out to either side like Theda Bara, as if she were trying to imprint her personality on me. She called her breasts her wings.'

'Jesus, how corny,' Vi commented. 'What a kook.'

'I can see that now,' Rose said. 'She studied Zen and karate and shaved her legs and armpits with a straight-edge razor. She said the books my foster father read me were romantic crap and that he was trying to make me weak like him. She was always bawling him out for not being successful and showing more manhood.'

'I'll bet,' Vi said, 'especially in bed.'

'She fussed a lot about my health and keeping clean and not getting infected and not touching myself or letting anyone touch me. But she was always touching me herself for inspection or instruction, especially my private parts (she called them, but they were anything but private to her, you can believe me). She made me do her exercises with her. And she was always quick to give me slaps, which always made my foster father wince, although he never did anything to stop her. She said I needed reminders – it was Zen. But every once in a while she'd snatch me up and hug me fiercely, holding me high as if I were some sacrifice, or as if she were trying to inspire and terrorise me at the same time. I was plain scared to death of her. As soon as she came near, I'd tighten up.'

Vi shook her head. 'The things they do to us, one way or another.'

'For a long while she scared me off of other children. I made up an imaginary playmate, a little girl exactly like me except her mother was dead.' Rose's eyes widened. 'Oh, Vi, do you suppose I somehow knew I had an identical twin? Or that there's been telepathy between us?'

'Could be,' Vi said thoughtfully, 'but maybe most imaginary playmates are like that.'

Rose continued, 'But eventually I got to have a real girl for a pal, a Black girl who was very slender and had narrow hands and long fingers like ours. I think she must have had Watusi blood. At first it was because she had a kitten. We'd play together on the way home. She loaned me Wonder Woman comics and Vampirella and Pantha.'

'I used to read those,' Vi said. 'Was Pantha the one who'd change into a black panther to destroy her parents and teachers and men who bothered her?'

'That's right. One dark afternoon we dared each other to go into a park we weren't ever supposed to. A storm was coming on but we kept daring each other to stay. It started to rain a little and we took shelter under some trees on a hilltop. Then thunder growled and the wind blew hard, tossing the leaves and branches, a siren started to wail down in the city, and we got this feeling that there were great dark wings over us. We both got very scared and held each other tight. And then it quieted down and we were touching each other.

'Oh God, Vi, to be touched with love! Not like my mother, as if you were something she owned and could handle exactly as she pleased, but something that's respected and understood and cherished.'

'I know,' Vi said softly, coming closer again, their hands lightly meeting. Rose went on, 'For a while then we were very happy, but what happened next, as you'd expect, was that my foster mother found out about our friendship. She was too smart to make it a racial thing – my foster father was very leftist in some ways – but that my little pal was light-fingered. She pretended to catch her stealing and called up her parents. There was a row and we were not allowed ever to see each other again. And then I found out that she'd also seen us touching and once kissing because she gave me an awful spanking to teach me, she said, never again to risk getting infected and that, although there was nothing wrong with Black girls, they could never help me to be successful.

'And after that she seemed almost to be more worried about girls touching me than boys. Of course it all put me off other kids again and I read a lot and even tried to write poetry and stories myself. That brought my foster father and me quite close for a while. He still read to me and we even talked about writing and things, although my foster mother watched us like a hawk and kept ranting about success and the main chance and how we both would be better off in mental hospitals.

'But she couldn't object to my next girlfriend (who came three years later) because she was from a wealthy Northshore political Irish family (her father was a state senator) and wore very expensive clothes and was white of course. My foster mother even tried to get palsy with her at first. But Siobhan could be very snotty in a ladylike way.

'Siobhan always had lots of spending money. With that and her hauteur she got us into adult and X-rated movies. Jane Fonda was our idol. We ate up *Klute* and *Barbarella* too. We romanced about becoming spacewomen and call girls. Under her snotty shell she was in many ways naïve as I and lonely too. One of us would pretend to be Snow White and the other would wake her. It was together that we learned French kissing and to pet to climax. And once we smoked some marijuana she'd snitched from her brother. I was wildly happy, but also very scared too from time to time – I'd get that dark wings feeling. Vi, would you be mad at me if I had some more brandy?'

'Of course not, Rose,' the other said. 'I'll have some too. To tell the truth, I was more shaken up at the window than I let on.'

'Why? What was it?' Rose demanded uneasily.

'At first the thing that was caught there seemed too big and yet somehow too insubstantial for a bird – as if it were a frantic invisible being in a cloak of bright black feathers.'

'Oh God! But it *was* a bird?'

'It was a bird,' Vi assured her. 'Here's our drinks – ah, that's better. Now how did your mother manage to wreck things this time?'

'She went to Siobhan's father at his office (she told me this when she confronted me) and made a big scene there, accusing Siobhan of corrupting me sexually and getting me on drugs and threatening to go to the other political party and their newspaper if he ever let Siobhan see me again. Of course he denied everything, but actually she'd hit on just the right way to throw a scare into him. Siobhan was taken out of school and sent to one in the East, I think. At any rate I never saw or heard from her again.

'And then my foster mother headed home, breathing fire, and confronted me with my foster father there, telling him his Little Miss Innocent and Fairy Princess was nothing but a dirty little lesbian bitch and demanding that he whip me with her razor strap and when he wouldn't, jeering at him and telling him then he could watch her do it.

'Oh God, Vi, it was awful. He pleaded with her, or rather he kept repeating that he didn't think it was wise or right – things like that – but, oh God, Vi, he didn't even try to stop her and he didn't run away, he stayed.'

'And you just stood still and let it happen,' Vi observed gently.

'No, Vi, I didn't,' Rose sobbed, tears spurting from her eyes. 'I fought hysterically then but – just as with you and your foster father – *she* was stronger. She twisted my wrist behind my back and forced me over, making it weirdly sexy, and then she whipped me. It hurt like hell, God how it hurt, there was some blood, but the worst thing almost was that I knew he was getting a thrill out of it. His little princess, and he was getting a thrill!'

'There, there, it's over,' Vi said soothingly, drawing Rose's head towards her shoulder.

'But it wasn't, Vi, that wasn't the worst,' Rose said, dry-eyed now, pulling away. 'After that happened I knew, like you, that I had to get out of there. And I guess my foster-father knew the same thing, because two days later he ran away with a young hippy woman it turned out he'd been having an affair with, but oh God, Vi, he didn't take me with him.

'I could have forgiven him being a coward and afraid to stop her – I was scared to death of her myself. I could even forgive him having sexual feelings seeing me whipped – I'd had sexual feelings myself, and not always at the nicest things, but oh God, Vi, he didn't take me with him! He ran away and didn't take me with him.'

Vi did not move to comfort her this time. Instead she studied her coolly and thoughtfully, missing nothing, not the track of one tear, as if Rose were an artist's model taking a pose and Vi the painter. Her pale blue eyes were at once sympathetic and merciless, and the distance within them was very great.

She said at last, 'Not to be loved, to find yourself betrayed . . . it's a very dry pain, isn't it? As if you were being tortured on the rack for witchcraft and then they stop, the instruments relax their poignant grip, the blinding light recedes, and the tormenting, endless, nagging questions come to an end.

'At first all that you feel is blessed numbness and a great enfolding silence. You think with quiet joy that perhaps you are dead at last.

'And then every last injury they've done you comes to excruciating life. There's the refinement of the cruelty – *they* don't have to do anything to you at that point; your body does it all, remembering. Yes, each hurt they've ever inflicted on you begins to throb unceasingly, the pitch mounting and mounting, until you think the agony can't become greater, but it does.

'And then you pray that they will start torturing you actively again – anything, *anything*, to disturb the embrace (as if it were a second skin) of that dry, fiery shroud.'

'You must have been there too,' Rose said quite quietly. 'Well, after my foster father ran away, my foster mother became quite insane in her hatred of all men . . . and of all girls too. She acted as if all the males in the world and every woman younger than herself, but especially the teen and subteen girls, the nymphets, were in a vast conspiracy against her. She kept threatening me with reform school and the mental hospital and she whipped me again.

'But then she overreached herself, thank God! – she really was crazy, Vi. She actually petitioned to have me sent to reform school as an uncontrollably wayward girl. I went to my high school English teacher, who'd encouraged me about my writing, and told her about it, and she brought in a social worker who was a friend. I still had the weals and cuts from the whipping and my foster mother went into a sort of fit in court. In the end I was put in a halfway house for girls with family problems like mine – or yours, Vi . . . fathers and brothers with incestuous tendencies.

'And for the next couple of years or so I lived a strange sort of half life there and in similar places (and really it's gone on – the limbo life – here in the Village too). They dunned my foster father and mother too for my support and got a little money from each of them from time to time, with difficulty, and they shifted me around between agencies.

'When I say half life, I mean in several ways. I came close to the edge, mentally, more than once. I was still basically a very shy child and my experiences made me shrink away from friendship. And after those whippings my mother gave me I just didn't have any sexual feelings at all for a long while. A doctor once told me that if the mind doesn't trust a sensory message coming from some part of the body, it registers it as pain – the panic reaction. So for that time most sexual feelings were actually painful to me – and frightening. A finger touching me would seem to burn – it's mixed up with my synesthesia, I'm sure.

'And then I was very mixed up as to how I felt about girls and sex generally. A couple of young women at the institution where I lived openly boasted about being lesbian, as if it were something very special, which didn't turn me on at all. I also knew that the people on whose good will I depended, even my English teacher, didn't approve of and wouldn't sympathise with that sort of thing at all. So I knew I had to hide any feelings like that and my experiences with my little Watusi and Siobhan.

'And all the while I was still terrified of boys, of course – I mean young men – and still am, you can believe me. Knowing it was my foster mother's strange teachings and my foster father's betrayal didn't change that one bit and never has. And that basic fear of mine was reinforced when a male counsellor tried to seduce me. He actually tried to use sleeping pills to help, Vi, can you imagine? And then a girlfriend here in NYC who'd said she was uncertain about which sex she was, fell for a man real hard and got the idea one night it would be real cute and a big favour to me if he introduced me to sex with men – whether under her active supervision or not I never learned. I almost panicked before I managed to get rid of them.

'Well, anyway, my English teacher stuck with me through all this, the darling! And as soon as I was barely old enough, helped me to get the job that I hold now. She thought I needed a change of city and she was right. I even inherited this apartment from an old friend of hers.

'So here I am, Vi, living my halfway life, making indexes, and trying to be a writer. I've just had a story rejected by *Cosmopolitan*, but they wrote a nice letter saying that it came close and asking me to keep submitting.'

'I've my ambitions too,' Vi said.

'Ballet?' Rose asked.

'In part,' Vi answered. 'But ultimately solo pantomime – concise, dramatic acts, historical, contemporary, and fantasy. My own costumes, settings, music – everything. There was a dancer and mime named Angna Enters. Something like hers.'

'That's wonderful,' Rose said. 'Maybe I could write acts for you.'

'I'm sure you could and maybe I could give you ideas for stories. Will you write one about tonight?'

'I don't know,' Rose said thoughtfully. 'Long lost twin sisters find each other – where's the conflict? It's all happy ending.'

'You'd have to work out a surprise premise for it,' Vi said rapidly, sitting up straighter. 'Suppose I were a young man who looked exactly like you – maybe identical twins of different sexes are possible this once. I have this overpowering lech for you, but I also know about your locks and bolts and fears. So I have my breasts injected. I even know about your mole and duplicate it –'

'Oh Vi!' Rose said reprovingly. 'That's just too complicated.'

'Well, if we *were* identical twins of different sex,' Vi argued, 'maybe I'd have female breasts too with the mirror-image mole, so I wouldn't need injections. Maybe only the primary sex organs would differ.'

'Stop it,' Rose said. 'I don't like that plot – it's too farfetched. Besides, you're thinking like your foster father.' Her hands moved as if she were going to button the top of her dress.

'I do believe I've frightened you again,' Vi teased, grinning a little.

'No, you haven't,' Rose denied, her hands dropping away. 'Remember, along with your breasts I've seen your nipples. It's just that I've gotten depressed. Reaction, I guess, or maybe the brandy. And then you start –' She broke off and impulsively moving closer, her arms hanging limp, her hands with palms upturned, said in a quavering, oddly tragic voice, 'Vi, comfort me.'

Vi did not move, except that her gaze wandered about Rose's face and shoulders, dropped to the supine hands, then travelled up to the woeful eyes again. She was smiling tenderly, but her own eyes had the distance in them.

There came that skirling cry, muffled this time, and (muffled too) a high, twanging sound, as of something sharp scraped across metal mesh. Rose started violently, wincing, then twisted around abruptly to look at the door. Vi got up then and moved towards it.

Rose followed her closely, hands trembling, but poised as if about to grab the other's shoulders, crying, 'Don't open it!'

Standing on tiptoes, Vi put her right eye to the fisheye lens set just above the little door-in-a-door masking the grille.

'I can't see anything,' she said coolly. 'The hall light must be out,' and unlatched the little door.

'Don't!' Rose said, clutching her shoulders now, but Vi opened it.

Another skirling cry, unmuffled, came knifing in and with it the brushing and beating of wings and the unnerving scrape of claws (or was it that?) on heavy wire.

'Still can't see anything,' Vi reported tersely. 'A black flashing –'

The sounds broke off except that of something like a huge but unsubstantial bird blindly brushing and buffeting about in the black hall.

'Please close it,' Rose implored. Vi did so.

Unmindful of Rose dragging her back, Vi said, 'I really should go out there –' Rose said, 'No, No!' '– though how that bird managed to get inside –' She looked at Rose and said reasonably, 'Well, should we call the apartment manager (there is one?) or the police?'

'The phone's disconnected,' Rose said miserably. 'I let the bill get too big.'

'So –?' Vi said quizzically (they could hear nothing now outside the door) '– well, we could scream.'

Rose answered, 'The room was soundproofed by an earlier tenant – my English teacher's friend.'

Vi smiled. 'Well, I suppose we could always open the windows wide and scream together –'

'Don't make fun,' Rose protested. 'Oh Vi, I'm so scared and miserable. You've just got to stay with me tonight. Oh Vi, comfort me. Take off your clothes and come to bed and comfort me,' she pleaded, clutching the other again and pressing her head between the other's neck and shoulder.

After a bit she heard Vi say tenderly but very deliberately, 'Very well, I will.' Then she felt her hands being gently but firmly disengaged and put to her sides and then she felt the pressure of Vi's palm in the small of her back, guiding her back to the low daybed.

'Sit down,' she heard and did so on the edge, looking at her stockinged knees. She heard Vi moving around. The lights went out. There were soft sounds. Then Vi returned and sat down close to her. The soft glow from the bathroom showed her Vi's dimly gleaming knees beside her own and she saw how alike they were. Then with a little sob that surprised her (she thought she'd quieted down) she turned to Vi, who'd left her singlet on, and clutched her, saying, 'Oh, Vi.'

'Be still,' she heard Vi calmly order her. 'How can I comfort you properly if you're crawling all over me?'

Again she felt her hands being gently but firmly disengaged, only this time Vi put them behind Rose's back and pinioned the wrists in her left hand.

Rose looked up shyly into Vi's ghostly face, the eyes dark smudges below the close-cropped head, neat as a bird's, and said, 'We've both got very long-fingered hands, only yours are stronger.'

'Is that bad?' Vi teased and then, nodding towards the books, 'You've read about it all in *The Joys of Sex*, I'm sure – bondage and discipline. Do you like it?'

'Unless it gets too scary,' Rose confessed, lifting up her face to kiss Vi's chin lightly.

'Well, as to that, one cannot tell ahead of time. We play by ear,' Vi said, giving her a soft peck between the eyes. Then her right hand went to Rose's brassiere. Pinching one cup between thumb and forefinger and the other between little finger and palm, she drew them together and used her middle finger to nudge loose the hook. She touched Rose's breasts in turn and leaned her cheek against them. Vi's eyelashes felt to Rose like a tiny bird fluttering. She felt Vi's hand trail down between her breasts and then finish unbuttoning her dress.

Vi lifted her face, smiling, and drawing Rose's arms a little farther down behind her back to expose her neck, gave her a gentle nip between the hinge of her jaw and her collarbone, and then again on the lobe of her ear, breathing humorously, 'Don't struggle – it won't help you. I'm the third vampire, remember?'

Rose felt quite frightened and yet not afraid, as if there were flashes of light on the verge of vision or at its edges, too faint to hurt or even to be seen. She felt adventurous.

Still holding her wrists tight, that arm against Rose's hip and garter belt, Vi slipped around and knelt on the carpet in front of her, very close to Rose (still on the edge of the low daybed) but with back so straight that her face was on a level with Rose's, even a little higher, her eyes flashing in the gloom.

Rose thought, 'I'm like Andromeda chained to the rock. Only the monster's friendly.'

As if Vi were reading her mind, she heard her say, 'It's fun to play with fears, now isn't it? You could safely imagine now that your twin's also a bird-woman, one of the archetypes even. The animus.'

Rose felt the spread fingers of Vi's right hand push into her hair and through it around the sides of her head to the nape of her neck and grip a large lock there (it pulled her scalp) and lift her face, bending it back a little, and then Vi kissed her mouth, her eyes, her cheek, her neck, her breasts. It took her breath away, she gasped, 'Oh God, oh Vi,' and seemed to hear, but only in her imagination, only playfully, the rush and beat of wings, the skirling cries, Vi's fingers velvet talons and her soft lips a beak.

She felt Vi press her body more closely against her own, front to front. She tried to push away, but Vi's strong left hand pinioning her wrists pressed them into the small of her back, against her coxyx, so that she couldn't move in that direction and the stockinged soles of her feet kept slipping on the carpet as they pushed frantically and finally kicked.

And then she felt (she experienced it as a point of intensely bright white light, shockingly painful) the unknown forcibly and irresistibly entering her between her legs.

She gasped, 'Oh no, oh no,' Vi whispered fiercely, 'There, there,' the point of light grew to an almost blinding white-hot moon that suddenly began to flash with scarlet. She squeezed her eyelids but it didn't stop, Vi's shrewd right hand closed alternately on her breasts, now left, now right, lightly pinching the nipples, her wrists and Vi's left hand pinioning them were like an iron knot at the base of her spine against which her body was jolting violently, there was a bitter taste at the base of her tongue and a brimstone stench high inside her nostrils, she heard Vi whisper, 'The ego is not inaccessible, you see,' and then she was seeing Vi through flashes of black light that made it seem as if her twin's slim dancer's body was covered with bright black feathers and the night itself was like great dark wings beating rhythmically, there was a skirling and deep booming in her ears, and Vi was saying through her devouring kisses in tones that kept gathering triumphant force, 'There, there; there, there; there *there*!'

GENERAL FICTION

		Cyril Abraham	
Δ	042697114X	THE ONEDIN LINE: THE SHIPMASTER	80p
Δ	0426132661	THE ONEDIN LINE: THE IRON SHIPS	80p
Δ	042616184X	THE ONEDIN LINE: THE HIGH SEAS	80p
Δ	0426172671	THE ONEDIN LINE: THE TRADE WINDS	80p
Δ	0352304006	THE ONEDIN LINE: THE WHITE SHIPS	95p
		Spiro T. Agnew	
	0352302550	THE CANFIELD DECISION	£1.25*
		Lynne Reid Banks	
	0352302690	MY DARLING VILLAIN	85p
		T. G. Barclay	
	0352304251	A SOWER WENT FORTH	£1.95
		Michael J. Bird	
Δ	0352302747	THE APHRODITE INHERITANCE	85p
		Judy Blume	
	0352302712	FOREVER	75p*
		John Brason	
Δ	0352305355	SECRET ARMY: THE END OF THE LINE	75p
		Barbara Brett	
	0352303441	BETWEEN TWO ETERNITIES	75p*
		André Brink	
	0352305916	RUMOURS OF RAIN	£1.95
		Jeffrey Caine	
	0352302003	HEATHCLIFF	75p
	0352395168	THE COLD ROOM	85p
		Ramsey Campbell	
	0352304987	THE DOLL WHO ATE HIS MOTHER	95p*
	0352305398	THE FACE THAT MUST DIE	95p
	0352300647	DEMONS BY DAYLIGHT	95p*

BARBARA CARTLAND'S ANCIENT WISDOM SERIES

	Barbara Cartland	
0427004209	THE FORGOTTEN CITY	70p*
	L. Adams Beck	
0427004217	THE HOUSE OF FULFILMENT	70p*
	Marie Corelli	
0427004225	A ROMANCE OF TWO WORLDS	70p*
	Talbot Mundy	
0427004233	BLACK LIGHT	70p*
	L. Adams Beck	
0427004241	THE GARDEN OF VISION	70p*

† For sale in Britain and Ireland only.
* Not for sale in Canada. • Reissues.
Δ Film & T.V. tie-ins.

GENERAL FICTION

Δ	0426187539	R. Chetwynd-Hayes **DOMINIQUE**	75p
	0352303514	Magda Chevak **SPLENDOUR IN THE DUST**	£1.50*
Δ	0352395621	Jackie Collins **THE STUD**	85p
	0352300701	**LOVEHEAD**	95p
	0352398663	**THE WORLD IS FULL OF DIVORCED WOMEN**	75p
Δ	0352398752	**THE WORLD IS FULL OF MARRIED MEN**	75p
	0426163796	Catherine Cookson **THE GARMENT**	95p
	0426163524	**HANNAH MASSEY**	95p
	0426163605	**SLINKY JANE**	95p
	0352302194	Tony Curtis **KID ANDREW CODY AND JULIE SPARROW**	95p*
	0352396113	Robertson Davies **FIFTH BUSINESS**	£1.25*
	0352395281	**THE MANTICORE**	£1.25*
	0352397748	**WORLD OF WONDERS**	£1.50*
	0352301880	D. G. Finlay **ONCE AROUND THE SUN**	95p
	0352304073	**THE EDGE OF TOMORROW**	£1.25
	0352304995	Norman Garbo **THE ARTIST**	£1.50*
	0352395273	Ken Grimwood **BREAKTHROUGH**	95p*
Δ	0352304979	Robert Grossbach **CALIFORNIA SUITE**	75p*
Δ	035230166X	**THE GOODBYE GIRL**	60p*
	0352304359	Elizabeth Forsythe Hailey **A WOMAN OF INDEPENDENT MEANS**	£1.25*
Δ	0352305142	Peter J. Hammond **SAPPHIRE AND STEEL**	75p
	0352301406	W. Harris **SALIVA**	60p
Δ	0352304030	William Johnston **KING**	£1.25*

† For sale in Britain and Ireland only.
* Not for sale in Canada. ● Reissues.
Δ Film & T.V. tie-ins.

GENERAL FICTION

	0352303956	Heinz Konsalik **THE WAR BRIDE**	95p
	0427003210	**THE DAMNED OF THE TAIGA**	75p
	0352303883	**NATASHA**	95p
	0352304022	**THE CHANGED FACE**	95p
Δ	0352398981	Jeffrey Konvitz **THE SENTINEL**	70p*
	0352301643	Dean R. Koontz **NIGHT CHILLS**	85p*
	035230412X	Andrew Laurance **PREMONITIONS OF AN INHERITED MIND**	95p
	0352304154	Ellie Ling **THE FIRST SPLASH**	75p
	0352303328	Pat McGrath **DAYBREAK**	95p
Δ	0352396903	Lee Mackenzie **EMMERDALE FARM (No. 1) THE LEGACY**	70p
Δ	0352396296	**EMMERDALE FARM (No. 2) PRODIGAL'S PROGRESS**	70p
Δ	0352395974	**EMMERDALE FARM (No. 3) ALL THAT A MAN HAS . . .**	75p
Δ	0352301414	**EMMERDALE FARM (No. 4) LOVERS' MEETING**	70p
Δ	0352301422	**EMMERDALE FARM (No. 5) A SAD AND HAPPY SUMMER**	70p
Δ	0352302437	**EMMERDALE FARM (No. 6) A SENSE OF RESPONSIBILITY**	70p
Δ	0352303034	**EMMERDALE FARM (No. 7) NOTHING STAYS THE SAME**	75p
Δ	0352303344	**EMMERDALE FARM (No. 8) THE COUPLE AT DEMDYKE ROW**	75p
Δ	0352304103	**EMMERDALE FARM (No. 9) WHISPERS OF SCANDAL**	75p
Δ	0352304510	**EMMERDALE FARM (No. 10) SHADOWS FROM THE PAST**	75p
Δ	0352302569	**ANNIE SUGDEN'S COUNTRY DIARY (illus)**	£1.25
Δ	0352304340	**EARLY DAYS AT EMMERDALE FARM**	75p
Δ	0352304286	David Martin **MURDER AT THE WEDDING**	95p
Δ	0352396164	Graham Masterton **THE MANITOU**	70p*
	0352395265	**THE DJINN**	75p*
	0352302178	**THE SPHINX**	75p*
	0352395982	**PLAGUE**	95p*
	0352396911	**A MILE BEFORE MORNING**	75p*

† For sale in Britain and Ireland only.
* Not for sale in Canada. • Reissues.
Δ Film & T.V. tie-ins.

GENERAL FICTION

		Joan Morgan	
Δ	0352304367	**MARY BLANDY**	£1.50
	0352301562	N. Richard Nash **EAST WIND, RAIN**	95p*
	0352395060	**CRY MACHO**	95p*
	0352303778	**THE LAST MAGIC**	£1.50*
	0352302720	Anaïs Nin **DELTA OF VENUS**	£1.25*
	0352306157	**LITTLE BIRDS** (Export only Excluding Aust., N.Z., S.A.)	£1.10*
	0352303271	Alan Parker **PUDDLES IN THE LANE**	70p
	0427004470	Graham Parker **THE GREAT TROUSER MYSTERY** (Large Format)	£3.95
	0352300809	Molly Parkin **LOVE ALL**	75p
	0352397179	**UP TIGHT**	95p
	0352302631	**SWITCHBACK**	95p
	0352302151	**GOOD MOLLY MS MOLLY** (illus) NF	£1.25
	035230331X	**PURPLE PASSAGES** (illus poetry)	£1.25
Δ	0426189647	Larry Pryce **FINGERS**	60p
	0352398779	Fiona Richmond **FIONA (NF)**	75p
	0352303808	**THE STORY OF I**	75p
	0352305215	**ON THE ROAD**	75p
	0352305568	**THE GOOD, THE BAD AND THE BEAUTIFUL**	95p
	0352303913	Maria Isabel Rodriguez **THE OLIVE GROVES OF ALHORA**	75p
	0352303581	Jack Ronder **THE LOST TRIBE**	£1.50
	0352396946	Judith Rossner **TO THE PRECIPICE**	85p*
	0352302089	**NINE MONTHS IN THE LIFE OF AN OLD MAID**	75p*
	0352301465	**ANY MINUTE I CAN SPLIT**	95p*
	0352302135	Lawrence Sanders **THE PLEASURES OF HELEN**	95p*

† For sale in Britain and Ireland only.
* Not for sale in Canada. • Reissues.
Δ Film & T.V. tie-ins.

Wyndham Books are obtainable from many booksellers and newsagents. If you have any difficulty please send purchase price plus postage on the scale below to:

>
> **Wyndham Cash Sales**
> P.O. Box 11
> Falmouth
> Cornwall
>
> OR
>
> **Star Book Service,**
> G.P.O. Box 29,
> Douglas,
> Isle of Man,
> British Isles.

While every effort is made to keep prices low, it is sometimes necessary to increase prices at short notice. Wyndham Books reserve the right to show new retail prices on covers which may differ from those advertised in the text or elsewhere.

Postage and Packing Rate

UK: 30p for the first book, plus 15p per copy for each additional book ordered to a maximum charge of £1.29. **BFPO and Eire:** 30p for the first book, plus 15p per copy for the next 6 books and thereafter 6p per book. **Overseas:** 50p for the first book and 15p per copy for each additional book.

These charges are subject to Post Office charge fluctuations.